By

Stacey Brandon

&

Karen Bell

Fall

Book Two in The Crash Series

Cover Designer/Photography
Stacey Brandon Photography

Editing
Donnie Bell

Design and Formatting
Tyler Bell

Copyright © 2015
by
Stacey L. Brandon and Karen L. Bell

All rights reserved.

This book or any portion thereof may not be reproduced or used in any manner whatsoever without the express written permission of the publisher except for the use of brief quotations in a book review.

This book is a work of fiction. Names, characters, places, and incidents either are products of the author's imagination or are used fictitiously. Any resemblance to actual persons, living or dead, events, or locales is entirely coincidental.

The author(s) acknowledges the trademarked status and trademark owners of various products referenced in this work of fiction, which have been used without permission. The publication/use of these trademarks is not authorized, associated with, or sponsored by the trademark owner.

First Printing, 2016

ISBN 978-0-9967928-2-0

www.BrandonBellAuthors.com

First Edition

Dedications

We dedicate "Fall" to all our fellow "book whores".

We were blown away by the positive response to our first book, "Crash" and we love how so many of you fell in love with Charli and Logan.

We hope this book makes you find room in your heart to also love our Liv and Zac.

Happy Reading!

Contents

Chapter One: Liv
Off Limits

What in the hell is he doing here? Who is he?

"Liv? Are you okay?"

"What?" Forcing my eyes away from the bar's entrance, I turn to face Charli. She's my best friend and roommate, even though the roommate part will be changing soon. She obviously wants my attention but right now I'm focused on the latest arrival to her engagement party. I never thought I'd see him again.

Charli scans the room for an explanation for my strange behavior. "What just happened? Your mouth is hanging open and it's not a good look for you."

I clear my throat. "Remember the foundation's charity gala last year?" Watching her face contort in pain, I feel like shit for bringing up a night she wants to erase.

"I'm not likely to forget it. Is there a reason you want to discuss one of the worst nights of my life during a party to celebrate the best part of my life?" She puts both hands on her hips and pointedly taps the toe of one of her shoes.

Charli's shoes are midnight blue with five-inch heels that are shit hot, by the way. I picked them out and I have a wicked good sense of style.

I try to get back to the topic at hand. "Sorry. I know we are supposed to pretend that night never happened and all. It's just that..." I don't get to finish my explanation because I hear foot-steps coming up behind me. As I watch, Charli's smile explodes like the city's firework display. Obviously, her soon-to-be-hus-band - Logan - has decided to join us.

Sliding between us, Logan wraps his arms around Charli's slender waist and lifts her up for a kiss. "Hey, my little Chuck."

Charli is what we politely refer to as vertically challenged. I'm not exactly tall but she's exaggerating when she tries to con-vince people she measures five feet. And that big guy sucking her face in front of me... *gross*... is six foot two inches. To say they look odd together is like saying those Hemsworth brothers are a little cute. Regardless, the two of them are disgustingly in love and since I love them both, I put up with all the public displays of affection. Not for the first time, Charli and Logan are so wrapped up in their mutual admiration society, I've become invisible. It's a damn good thing I'm secure with myself or I could end up with self-esteem issues thanks to them.

It isn't long before I realize that I'm not the only person impa-tiently waiting out the love fest. A deep, loud clearing of a throat behind me finally persuades Logan and Charli to disengage their mouths, even though she stays closely nestled under his arm.

"Oh...sorry!" Charli grins with a flush of embarrassment while Logan just looks damn proud of himself.

Shaking my head at the two of them - *I've reached my limit of mush* - I spin around and come face to chest with a dark blue dress shirt and gray patterned tie. Raising my chin up, and then even farther up, I encounter the underside of a strong jawline. Clean shaven, but dark enough to suggest a razor will be needed again soon, there's a strong cleft in the chin and I inhale sharply with recognition. *It's him.*

Dark, thick hair tops an angular face that I itch to photograph. *That bone structure!* His warm chocolate eyes are heavy lidded and lazily sexy but the thin silvery scar bisecting his left eyebrow leaves me no doubt that it's him. He's my idea of male perfection. Even though he and I have never been introduced, this beautiful stranger has unknowingly played a starring role in many of my fantasies over the past year.

Taking a small step back, I try to give him a normal amount of personal space. *What I really want to do is share his personal space.*

He smiles, one side pulling up higher than the other, and puts his hand forward. "Hello." The deep smoothness of his voice makes me forget how to breathe. *What the fuck is wrong with me?* I don't get nervous around guys...I make them nervous. I've been told that I'm an acquired taste but I've always taken it as a compliment. *Who wants easy and uncomplicated? That would be boring.*

I continue standing in front of him with hands hanging limply at my side and mouth slack. I have to accept that for the first time, I can't think of a single thing to say.

"Zac!" Logan booms, saving me. "I want you to meet Liv. She's the one I told you about." My best friend's fiancé comes over, standing right next to this god among mortals and looks at me expectantly.

I think I'm supposed to be doing something now. *What in*

the hell am I supposed to be doing?

"Liv?" Charli comes closer and elbows me hard enough to push my fog of lust away a little...a very little.

"Damn," I breathe out and the guys erupt in laughter. Charli cringes but she knows me well enough that she shouldn't be surprised. My mom says I was born without the ability to filter my words. My other mom is sure it's a learned habit I picked up from her. I feel like this is an asset. I don't bullshit people.

I drag out all the social niceties my poor mom has tried to instill in me. "It's nice to meet you, Zac" I manage to spit out. For my friend's sake, I try to appear nice and normal. Hopefully, I'm pulling it off, but when I put my hand out and it disappears into his, I have to keep reminding myself it's not polite to ask someone you just met if you can see them naked.

There's a twinkle in the bottomless depths of his eyes and I find myself desperately needing to swallow. "You too, Liv." He then twists to the side and pulls someone out from behind him. He puts his arm around her. "This is my fiancé, Sabrina."

Fuck me. Of course, she is.

"Logan has told us so much about you!" Sabrina gushes with a wide smile and perfect teeth. I have to look up to see her and I take in the straight, chestnut hair, deep-set hazel eyes, and dark beauty I guess to be of Latin American descent. She is beautiful and she looks very happy to meet me. She wouldn't be happy if she knew what I was dreaming of doing with... *and to*... the man beside her only a few moments ago.

I smile back because it's not her fault I'm hot for her soon-to-be-husband. "Well, if you are marrying Logan's childhood friend... then I'm happy to report he has at least mentioned you exist." I pat Logan's back for a job well done, and they laugh. Logan had told me one of his groomsmen was looking for a wedding

4

photographer and that he'd recommended me but never in a million years could I have imagined that his friend in need would be the guy I've wanted to find for almost a year.

"Yeah, that sounds right," Zac says, shaking his head. "Logan and I haven't seen each other much since he moved away from our hometown but now that Sabrina and I have moved to the city, I'm hoping that changes."

"Oh, you live here now?" *I'm not supposed to be happy to hear this, right?*

"Zac is opening a new restaurant," Logan explains.

I look at Zac. "Cool. I like to eat." *I'm a fucking idiot.*

Zac chuckles. "Good to know," he assures me with a mock seriousness. "We've seen some of your photography, by the way. You're very talented."

"Thanks." *Why can't I hold a normal, rational conversation this evening?*

"We want to set up engagement pictures pretty soon if you have time?" Sabrina chimes in. "I'd really love a bridal shoot closer to the big day and of course, we want you for the actual wedding."

"Uh... Sure. Yeah, I can do that. I can give you my number and we can set it up. Sounds great." *It sounds like a fucking nightmare.*

Sabrina waves a hand dismissively in my direction. "Oh, Logan gave me your number already so I'll call you next week, if that's good with you?"

I give her a thumbs up. "Perfect. Can't wait." What I can't wait for is making my escape and heading back to the bar for another drink. *And why did I give her a thumbs up? Who does that?*

Sabrina smiles at me again. *Damn, she really is beautiful. Damn, she seems really nice too.* I want to hate her, obviously because I'm so damn jealous of her at the moment, but she's mak-

5

ing it hard.

"Great!" she says, and then I watch her tilt her head up and give Zac a quick kiss. He smiles down at her with complete adoration and love.

I'm sure Sabrina and Zac will have a lovely wedding, a lovely life, and lovely babies. I'll just keep going out on horrendous blind dates, set up by my so-called friends, Kelly, and Scott. My choices haven't worked out so well, so I'd agreed to let them set me up a few times... but their options are making me seriously consider a convent. The problem is, black really washes me out. Plus, giving up my three-tiered, aluminum lock box of makeup and having to forgo shit hot heels for sensible shoes, would never work out for me. I won't even get started on the vow of celibacy.

"It was really great to finally meet you," Zac says with a knowing smile that makes me fear he can read my mind. Although if he could, he would probably be asking for a restraining order.

"Uh huh," I finally manage to answer, because that's how I'm rolling tonight. I'd like to kick my own ass for sounding so stupid.

"I'll call you soon!" Sabrina reminds me with a quick wave, before taking her personal hunk of gorgeous by the arm and heading toward the bar.

I already knew he was eye candy, but did he have to be funny and have his shit together too? Why couldn't he have made my life easier by being a douchebag with Mommy issues?

I like to talk big but I'm not a home wrecker and never will be. I resign myself to the fact that Zac is completely off limits. It sucks but that's life sometimes.

Knowing I will never pursue him, I allow myself one last look. Maybe he feels my stare - *it's always possible I have some superhero powers* - because he turns his head and we lock eyes. At first, he smiles but then his brow furrows and he frowns slightly.

Shit. I must not be smiling back. Am I drooling? I break our connection and turn away from him… and right into Charli.

"What's going on, Liv?" Her voice is concerned and I know she stayed back to talk to me. It's not as though she wouldn't have noticed I was acting strange… well stranger than normal. We've been best friends our whole lives. There's no point in trying to pretend nothing just happened.

"Well," I sigh, hating to once again bring up that awful evening but not seeing a choice. "I know you remember the charity event last year as the night you and Logan broke up… over the confusion with Victoria…" She cringes with the echo of hurt. It had been a misunderstanding but at the time, Charli had believed Logan was cheating on her and it had broken her heart. They resolved everything but I know she still hates to talk about it.

"Yeah, that wasn't a good one for us."

"I know and I'm sorry to mention it but do you remember that before everything went to shit, I saw a really hot guy? You made fun of me for trying to get his attention and… rude ass bitch that you are… even laughed at me when I got pissed he was with a date."

"Oh, yeah!" She laughs. "I've never seen you try so hard! And you wouldn't let me turn around and check out 'Mr. Tall, Dark, and Handsome', in case he noticed us watching him and then…" Realization floods her face and her laughter withers.

"It was him? It was Logan's friend Zac?" Her voice ratchets up a few notches and I threaten to strangle her if she doesn't shut the fuck up.

"Yep. What are the odds?"

"Wow," she whispers, "I can't believe it. I remember you saying the guy had a scar through his eyebrow and I was impressed you noticed something like that from such a distance but I never really got a look at him. When Logan introduced me to Zac last week, I never connected it. Why would I? It has been so long. This is so weird..." She shakes her head but then looks over at me with pity.

"Stop it, Charli," I demand. "It caught me off guard but it's not that big of a deal. I don't even know him. I'll admit he's amazingly hot and I'm disappointed I didn't get a chance to have a go at him but cheating is something I'll never do."

"I know that, Liv," she tells me softly. "You like to act like you're such a badass bitch but you are a good person."

"Whatever," I roll my eyes at her. *I have a reputation to uphold, after all.* "Besides, we'd probably end up completely hating each other and that would put Logan in an awkward position. And maybe he has a small dick."

Charli snorts with amusement, as I'd intended, and finally lets it go. It doesn't matter if we could have made each other ecstatically happy or tragically miserable. He's about to marry someone else.

Chapter Two: Zac
Her Body Would Stop Traffic

"So, I know most people around here use the botanical gardens or the big stone columns in front of the University for their engagement pictures... but after I spoke on the phone with Sabrina, I thought you two would prefer this," she tells me.

The dirt path we've been following suddenly opens wide and disappears. What lies before us causes me to stop and appreciate how beautiful nature can be. Acres of open fields, with natural grasses and wildflowers as high as my knees, are bathed in the warm gold of late afternoon.

"Wow," I breathe out in awe. I had been hesitant when Liv explained the engagement shoot would require a little hike but I'm glad we decided to trust her.

"It's perfect, Liv. Thank you," Sabrina says before sliding her warm hand into mine and giving it a quick squeeze. Her beautiful smile of gratitude is directed at our photographer.

Liv's face is content and there's a hint of a smile as she surveys her chosen location with us. "I'm glad you like it." She had obviously paid attention to what we wanted.

We spend a few minutes changing out of the shoes we'd worn for the trek here and letting Sabrina touch up her hair and makeup. The weather has been a little cold all week but it's pleasant today and the walk required to get us here has made me comfortably warm. There had been a few issues finding a day that worked with all of our schedules so I'm doubly glad the weather is cooperating.

Sabrina has been stressing for the last couple of weeks about the shoot and she probably drove Liv crazy with all her questions. I must have heard "Liv says..." a hundred times in the last few days alone. It has started with, "Liv says the whole 'matching' this is overdone and expected. It's better to be coordinating." Sabrina had rummaged through the complete contents of our closets, quickly given up on anything we already owned, and then gone shopping for the perfect outfits.

So today, I'm in dark jeans and a gray button up shirt with a thin navy vertical stripe while Sabrina is rocking a short dress of mustard yellow with a navy belt and cardigan. She doesn't usually wear dresses but it's a spectacular choice to show off her legs that go on for miles.

Once we pass Liv's critical inspection, she puts her camera bag down and asks us to follow her a little farther into the field. "Okay guys, I want you to stand right here, leaning into each other," she says while adjusting a strand of Sabrina's long hair and picking a small piece of grass off the shoulder seam of my shirt.

"Where should we look?" Sabrina asks her.

"At each other," Liv says. "Don't look at me until I tell you to." Liv then looks directly at me and I feel my pulse accelerate. "I want you to just forget I'm even here."

I'm not sure that's possible.

I'm completely in love with Sabrina, I adore almost everything about her and most of all, I have no desire to be unfaithful. I'm not that kind of man. But, I am still a man and I'm not blind.

Liv draws attention, no matter the circumstances. While Sabrina is tall, thin and toned from hours in the gym, Liv is tiny, soft and feminine with that hourglass shape usually only found in fantasies. She's wearing black pants with a high waist, a leopard print blouse that's sheer enough for the sun to filter through and reveal the black tank top underneath, and red wedge-heeled sandals.

Who else but this woman could get away with wearing heels in the middle of nowhere?

Most women would look ridiculous. She looks amazing and has the vibe of the quintessential forties pinup babe. If I looked into a history book and saw her likeness on the nose of a bomber plane, it wouldn't surprise me at all. She's all curves and womanly confidence and it's sexy as hell. I'm actually curious to know if God gave her that shape or if she's had a little help from a scalpel, but how could I ask something like that?

And, it's none of my damn business anyway.

If you can get past the body that would stop traffic, her face is pretty damn amazing too. She has creamy, flawless skin, bright green eyes that sparkle with mischief, and that shocking red hair. Her hair is so intensely Technicolor that everything in its vicinity seems faded and washed out. She's impossible to miss.

I sound like some kind of asshole that objectifies women!

I comfort myself with the knowledge that there are lots of other things about Liv I can appreciate too. She's intelligent, talented, and has a sharp sense of humor. She's also in the habit of littering her conversations with unique profanities. Talking with her reminds me of poker night with the boys sometimes, but somehow she pulls it off with class.

What are the odds that I would see her again and, even more strange, that she would be the best friend of the woman Logan is marrying?

I haven't had the nerve to tell Logan that I'd actually seen Liv once before. Almost a year ago, I'd come into the city to scout locations for my future restaurant and while here, Sabrina and I had attended a charity dinner. Liv had been there.

"How is the restaurant coming along?" Liv asks, pulling me back to the present.

"Good. We've finalized most of the big decisions and I'm interviewing staff right now," I tell her.

"That's great. I know Logan is glad you've moved here."

"We love it," Sabrina tells her. "It was perfect timing too. I used to work at a small local gym in our hometown. When a position became available here in the city at one of the large chain fitness centers, I knew I had to take it. Now, instead of just teaching some classes, I am getting to do personal training and also work with the manager on scheduling and promotions."

Liv winks at Sabrina. "No wonder your body rocks! I'm always saying I should really drag my ass to the gym but I have this serious, ongoing love affair with sleep. I might also be a lazy bitch, according to Charli."

"Well, if you decide to give it a try you should definitely let me know. I'd love to help you," Sabrina assures her.

"Probably not going to happen, but thanks." Liv smiles and Sabrina smiles back while shaking her head. Sabrina loves to help "gym virgins."

I think back, again, to that night I'd seen Liv. She'd been in a green dress and laughing. She'd taken my breath away.

"Zac!" Sabrina says with frustration while poking me with her index finger.

"What? I'm smiling!" *I think I'm smiling. Am I smiling?*

"Yes... you are smiling," she says with a frown. "You aren't supposed to be smiling right now."

"Oh, sorry." Well, that's embarrassing. Liv probably thinks I'm an idiot.

I am an idiot. I need to be worrying about what Sabrina is thinking, not the woman here to take our engagement photos.

"I know pictures aren't exactly your idea of fun but babe, can you please try? This is important to me," Sabrina says. She doesn't nag or ask a lot of me, so my guilt escalates.

I pull her in tight against my side and kiss her temple. She's very tall for a woman, almost six foot actually, but I've still got four inches on her so I don't have to bend down far. "I know and I'm sorry. I've had a lot on my mind lately but that's no excuse."

I look over at Liv. With arms crossed under her ample chest, and one eyebrow arched, her patience looks like it's running thin. I wonder what expression she'd have if she knew that a memory of her had been the delay.

"We ready now, Zac?" Her voice is sweet condescension and I laugh. She'd keep a guy on his toes.

"Yeah, I'm good. Let's do this." Both girls laugh as I jump around, rubbing my hands together like I'm preparing for the big fight.

They are both so uniquely beautiful in their own way and my eyes don't know where to rest.

Chapter Three: Liv
Danger! Abort Mission!

Grabbing the handle, I pull open the heavy, slatted door to reveal a vestibule with scarred oak flooring and exposed brick walls. The future hostess stand looks as though it's made of reclaimed lumber and the glass pendant lights give a dim warmth that invites you in. It's unpretentious but elegant and I immediately love it.

"Hello?" I call out. I'm only ten minutes, *okay maybe it's closer to twenty minutes late...* but surely they haven't given up on me? If they'd left, wouldn't the front door be locked?

"Hello?" I try again, a little louder. Still nothing.

I see an arched opening to the right and step through and down onto a floor of etched and stained concrete. The artificial lights are minimal, and completely unnecessary since the whole space is flooded with brilliant sunlight from the giant, multi-paned windows that wrap around the whole dining space.

Through those windows, I see a courtyard filled with trailing ivy, lush greenery and small empty pockets of space I assume will soon house outdoor dining options. There are no tables or chairs. Stacks of crates line the far wall but I see enough to know that if this new restaurant's food is half as good as its design, it will be a huge success.

"Hey, Sabrina? Zac? Anyone here?" I call out loudly, my voice echoing through the silent room.

Walking out from a small door at the back, Mr. Sexy himself comes toward me with a smile that makes me moan under my breath with frustration. *It is so unfair I can't have him.*

His sleeves are rolled up to above the elbow as he dries his hands on a white muslin dishcloth and motions me toward the bar near the back of the room. "Liv! Glad you made it. Sorry, I didn't hear you earlier, I was in the back washing and checking all the new glassware." He sets the cloth down and pulls out a tall, high-backed barstool for me. "Sabrina is on the phone with her boss but she'll be out in just a minute. Can I get you anything to drink?"

"No. I'm good. Thanks, though." Setting the folder down, I jump a little to be able to slide onto the upholstered seat and I see him try to hide a smirk. I'd like to remind him that we can't all be damn Amazons, but thankfully catch myself in time. Biting my tongue, I let it go. Charli would be so proud of my restraint.

"I've brought the engagement portraits," I tell him, trying hard to ignore how close he is as he leans in to get a peek at the folder I'm carrying. "I'm really pleased with how they turned out and hope you and Sabrina like them." Being professional is such a bitch. *Why can't I just tell him they are a shit hot couple, I'm a fucking amazing photographer, and they better love these pictures like I do?*

His dark eyes twinkle and I worry he is reading my mind.

"Great! Let's see them." He reaches for the folder but I pull it away before our hands can make contact.

"Shouldn't we wait for Sabrina?" Experience has taught me that it's usually the women in charge of the order and letting the guy get the first peek can be met with mild aggravation or even outright hostility.

"I'm coming!" Sabrina's voice echoes across the vaulted room as she jogs up to us from a door in the far corner that probably leads to an office. I'm glad her arrival has saved me from needing delay tactics.

Pulling the prints out of the rigid folder, I spread them across the bar. I've printed eighteen proofs, my favorites, and I feel that familiar tingle of pride as I look at each one with them. From simple candid shots in beams of sunlight to bold close-ups in high contrast black and white, the pictures radiate love without any self-consciousness. These images tell a story of trust and caring. They tell a story I long to experience.

"Oh my God," Sabrina sighs out so softly I barely hear her. "They are perfect."

I can't begin to explain the way it feels when someone truly appreciates my art. I don't want people to look at their picture and just think they look good or how nice the photo will look hanging in their living room. I want people to feel something even when they can't pinpoint what it is. Sabrina's face shows this intangible reaction and I start to smile. She gets it.

Zac wraps his arm around her but turns his face toward me. His smile is sweet and appreciative... and it makes me inhale sharply. I'm suddenly aware of the staccato rhythm of my heart. I've known men that were beautiful or cute or insanely hot, but this man is all of those and something more. Just looking at him physically affects me. My body wants to respond even when my mind knows I shouldn't.

It's not that I'm appreciating his beauty as an artist would, although I am. It's not that I'm lusting for him as a woman does, although that's true too. It's something more. I know it's completely irrational and it scares me. It hurts knowing that this man is the first guy to ever make me feel like there's a real chance of me finding something more than superficial fun... and I can't have him. Maybe if he were single and I could act on my attraction, I'd discover we don't really work together, but the frustration of not knowing and only guessing at the possibilities is killing me.

His smile of gratitude starts to slip and we just stare at one another, with no expression and no words. Our eyes are locked into place, wordlessly saying something that they shouldn't be.

Danger! Abort Mission! For the love of all that is holy... Look away, Olivia Marie Garrett!

"Oh Zac, don't you just love them?" Sabrina's voice shatters our connection and I'm finally able to pull my eyes away from his. Even more importantly, I resume breathing. I should have been able to manage this on my own, breathing is an involuntary action after all, but instead, I needed an intervention. *I'm weak and useless. What in the hell is wrong with me?*

"Yes. Perfect." His voice is strained and I'm petrified he's witnessed too much in my eyes.

Shit. If he knows I have the hots for him, or worse, if he thinks that I'm trying to hit on him, then you can just shoot me now.

Searching for something else to say or do, I adjust my purse strap, play with the now empty folder, and eventually scoot down off the stool. "Okay...uh..." I've never been the type to become tongue tied but every time I'm around him my IQ plummets. *This sucks.*

Sabrina comes toward me and my first impulse is to flee but I hold my ground. *Keep it together, Liv! She can't read minds!* At least, I hope not.

Instead of slapping me, which I sort of feel like I deserve, she bends down and wraps her arms around me. I have personal space issues but I feel so guilty I decide to allow this intrusion. When she starts squealing and jumping around, with me still caged against her, I've had enough. Gently, I pry her off, smiling the whole time so as not to offend her, and sort of pat her shoulder in acknowledgment of her joy.

"Okay, great. Perfect. Glad you love them." I talk to her like I'm trying to placate a violent mental patient. It's time to get out of here. "You can just call me later with any additional prints or enlargements... or whatever." I start to back away...slowly.

"Do you have to go already?" she whines. "Zac was about to whip us up something to eat. Please stay."

"Ummm," I sneak a glance over to Zac and see his shoes are commanding his full attention.

Shit. He knows I weirded out and he just wants me gone.

"Tell her, Zac," Sabrina commands, "We'd both love for you to stay, Liv."

Does she think I don't notice her elbowing him?

"Oh, yeah," he abruptly adds, then his voice drops and when I find the nerve to raise my eyes toward him, there is softness in his mouth and a gentleness in his expression. "I make a mean spinach ravioli, Liv. Stay."

I want to stay. I really, really want to stay. And that's how I know, I have to leave. "Sounds delish but I'm meeting Charli and Logan, so..." I try again to extricate myself by backing up a small step.

"I understand," he assures, but he looks hurt.

How can he understand? I don't understand anything at this point. All I know is that what I want to do and what I need to do are at war with one another.

"Tell them hello for us," Sabrina says and I turn to look at her in confusion.

"Who?" I ask her. I'm so rattled right now and she's not making any sense.

"Charli and Logan! You said you had plans with them?" Now she's talking to me like *I'm* the mental patient. Maybe I should be.

"Oh!" *Shit, Liv... get it together before she figures out you're infatuated with her man.* "Charli and Logan... yep, we have plans. I'll tell them. I'll tell them you said hi and stuff."

"Thanks," she says with a little laugh. "I'd appreciate that."

"Absolutely." Pivoting away, about to finally be allowed those additional steps needed to escape, I feel Sabrina's hand on my shoulder stopping me.

Shit, I've been found out!

"I have an incredible idea!" she blurts out with cheerleader-worthy enthusiasm. She's even bouncing lightly from one foot to the next. "We were just discussing artwork for the bar area and the vestibule. We really want some black and white photographs that are representative of our style. There's this local farmer's market that Zac loves and uses for the majority of his fresh ingredients..." She turns her face back toward him with an encouraging expression and he nods at her and then looks to me.

"She's right," he says. "Liv, I'd really love for you to take the photographs for me. I was thinking pictures of the stalls, the produce and even some of the people milling about. I'd want a couple of large prints for the entrance, maybe one behind the bar, and then a row of four or five to go along the back wall. Just simply framed, so the work stands out. Would you be interested?"

I want to do this.

It sounds fun and different and what an incredible opportunity to have my art seen by so many people.

Can I do this?

Can I get past whatever fantasies I've cooked up about a man I don't know very well, a man that belongs to someone else and can never be mine, and just be strong enough to put my career first?

I will not let this temporary "lust-itis" - *that's totally a thing and they need to develop an antibiotic for it* - get the better of me or ruin this chance. And I really do like both Sabrina and Zac. They are a great couple. Whatever glitch I'd experienced a few minutes ago - *okay it's been going on a lot longer but regardless* - it was just a figment of my imagination, fueled by exhaustion and some bad tacos at lunch. *I need to quit letting Charli pick where we eat.*

"I am very interested. Thank you."

"No, thank you," Sabrina insists. "Let's find a day soon so we can all go together and show you our favorite spots."

"Okay. Perfect." My voice is firm and confident. I smile first at Sabrina and then at Zac. When he smiles back and reaches forward, my hand disappears into both of his. The electric tingle that runs up my arm from the contact makes my eyes close involuntarily and I think I even sigh. My body has betrayed me again. My earlier confidence fades and is replaced by a bone-deep anxiety at knowing how hard the next several months will be for me.

"Perfect." He agrees.

Chapter Four: Zac
Nice Melons

"Are you sure you can't make it?" Hiding my disappointment isn't easy but I know it isn't her fault. Sabrina would be here if she could but her job is still new and she's determined to become indispensable.

"I'm so sorry, Zac. Allison called in sick at the last minute and I'm the only one that knows the routine well enough to teach her class. I'll need to cover her personal training clients too. And you know the weekend classes are always full and canceling this one, in particular when we are trying to increase our class rosters, would be disastrous." Even through the phone, I pick up on her guilt and if anyone can understand the demands of your career, it should be me.

"I know. I just thought today would be fun. I'll miss you."

"I'll miss you more. Give my apology to Liv. I wish I could be spending the day with you two but I know you'll have a great time and the weather is beautiful. Oh... and don't forget to pick me up some fresh berries and kale for my smoothies."

"Okay. Got it."

"I love you," she tells me.

"I love you too." I grin into the phone. We've been together since high school but I still can't wait for her to be Mrs. Sabrina Reynolds.

"Oh, I've got to go. It's almost time to start class. Bye!"

"Bye." I hang up and slide the phone back into the pocket of my jeans. Liv is already fifteen minutes late but our past meetings have proven this isn't an uncommon occurrence. At least, the weather is warm and the sky is clear so my wait is enjoyable.

I watch a couple of young kids begging, with the volume of wild banshees, for their frazzled mother to buy them a cookie at a nearby stall and it makes me think of my little brother Michael. He loves cookies and if he were here to see the rows of giant glass jars, lined up and filled with every flavor imaginable, his persistence would put these two to shame. He's hard to deny under any circumstances but when he sets his stubborn mind to something, God help anyone that tries to interfere. I decide to walk over and buy him a few.

"Would you like a sample?" A thin teenage girl with a bright smile asks enthusiastically.

"Sure." She hands me a napkin with a selection of small pieces of different cookies. They're delicious.

"I'll take a chocolate chip with walnuts, two peanut butter, and two sugar. Oh, and throw in a couple of snickerdoodles. They're my dad's favorite," I tell her. I know my mom would rather I bring her some fresh fruits and vegetables but this purchase will be a big hit with my dad and little brother. They love sweets. It was from my mom that I gained my love of cooking

22

and appreciation for fresh, sustainable ingredients but she'll like the cookies too.

"Here you go...Enjoy!" the girl behind the table tells me as she hands me a waxed paper bag sealed with a label that reads, 'Benny's Baked Goods.'

Maybe I should contact them and offer their cookies at the restaurant? They really are great and would be a nice option to go along with my more elaborate desserts.

Carrying my purchase, I think about the quick trip home I'm planning for tomorrow. I miss my family and even though it's only a two-hour drive, it's been difficult to find the time to make the trip lately.

Everywhere I look are the sights and sounds of vendors hawking their fresh, natural products and the crowds of excited people taking advantage of the variety of goods. It's just a simple hum of activity for the most part, until a loud and appreciative whistle slices through the peaceful drone.

Turning around to investigate, it becomes immediately clear what has inspired this universally understood show of male appreciation. Strolling my way, in a sundress the color of the Caribbean ocean, a wide brimmed straw sun hat, and bright yellow sandals... is Liv. Every man she passes stares with undisguised want and even the women watch her with envy or admiration or both. It's not just that she's a hot girl in an attention-getting outfit, she has a confidence that draws people to her. Sabrina and I had discussed this the other evening after she'd met with us at the restaurant.

"She's confident and sure of herself without being a self-absorbed bitch. That's so rare," Sabrina had said.

"Yeah, she's great," I'd agreed.

"I'd give anything to have a rack like hers," she'd admitted.

"Do you think they're real?"

"I like your rack just as it is, Sabrina," I'd assured her. "Come here and I'll show you how much I appreciate it." I'd pulled her into my arms and then taken her to our bedroom to prove my point. It had been a good night.

I look up again and see that Liv has noticed me. She waves and we split the distance to meet.

"Hey, Zac. Where's Sabrina?" Her voice is cheerful and she looks bright eyed and ready for adventure. I hope she loves this place like I do. I want her to feel inspired to create images that make you feel like you're here too, but I also want her to have fun.

"She can't make it because of work," I tell her. "So it looks like it's just us today."

Startled, she jerks back slightly and widens her eyes. Her smile fades and I find myself wondering if she disappointed. I really thought we'd hit it off and that she wouldn't mind hanging out with me but maybe she only likes Sabrina. *Have I done something to offend her?*

"Is that okay?" I ask hesitantly. She makes me nervous. I really want her to like me. I know Logan and Charli adore her and talk about how great she is all the time.

"Of course!" she says with a smile, so I try to relax.

"Can I carry your bag for you?" She doesn't have a lot of equipment, just a small bag from which she pulls out a heavy looking camera with a short stubby lens.

"I got it. Thanks, though. I'm just shooting with my 50mm/1.2 today. Have to love a prime, right? So, my bag is light."

I laugh at her. "Okay. Am I supposed to understand that?"

"Nah, you can leave the brains to me. You'll just be my pretty assistant." She lifts her nose up slightly and cocks a condescending eyebrow at me.

I grin. "I feel more like Igor next to you."

Liv narrows her eyes and purses her full lips in an adorable pout. "Are you calling me Dr. Frankenstein?" She raises her index finger in my direction. "Because, you should know that if you are... I'm actually kind of cool with that. Just because Frankenstein's monster was hideous, didn't mean the good doctor couldn't rock a pair of shit hot heels."

"What exactly makes a pair of shoes classify as 'shit hot heels'?" I know we are teasing, but I'm still curious what she'll answer.

"It's an indefinable quality actually. When you see them, you just know." She says this in a lowered tone, likes she's handing over state secrets.

She smells sweet and floral and I'm sort of paralyzed. Then she puts a foot forward to allow my eyes to travel from the dress hem that hits right above her knee and down the side of her well-defined calf to stop at her foot. Her toes, in a shade that exactly matches her dress, peek out of the front of the shoes and I understand her criteria exactly.

"Well," I swallow hard and look away. "Where should we begin?" Spinning around slowly, I look for possibilities. "We could head over to the produce or the baked goods... or maybe you'd like the floral carts?" Everything is exploding with color and activity.

"Show me your favorites," she requests softly. Her voice feels intimate and suddenly I'm thinking about how she'd make an amazing phone sex girl.

Shit! What in the hell is wrong with me? How can I even think something like that? Looking away in guilt, even though I know she can't be aware of what I was imagining, I try to get myself under control.

Personally, I've never understood the allure of getting off to anonymous women's voices. I don't know why that's what came to my mind when she was speaking but it feels sexist and humiliating. Maybe she senses my "inner perv" and that's why she wanted Sabrina here.

I want Sabrina here.

"Thirsty?" I indicate a stall behind me with glass beverage dispensers sweating in the day's warmth. "The organic ginger mint lemonade is the best."

Walking over, I give the guy at the table a couple of dollars and he hands me a clear plastic cup. I fill it from the jar of pale yellow liquid with floating leaves of mint and hand it to her.

"Thanks." She lifts the cup to her mouth, takes a small experimental sip, and then runs the tip of her tongue over the moisture that sticks in her glistening pink lip gloss.

"Well, it doesn't suck," she concedes and I laugh, "but cherry lemonade is my favorite. I love almost everything cherry flavored." Then she tilts her head back slightly and takes a longer, deeper drink.

Maybe it's time to move on.

"What made you get into photography?" I ask as we walk toward a table of homemade candles.

"I've always loved art and I used to draw and paint a lot. When I turned sixteen, my moms bought me a really great camera, thinking I would love it," she explains.

"I'll bet you did!"

"No, actually I hated it!" She laughs as she admits this.

"So, you decided to make a career out of something you hate?" I can't help but grin at her as she smells several mason jar candles and wrinkles her nose in disgust.

"Not exactly. I knew what I wanted my final images to look

like but I didn't have the skills to make it happen. A good camera can't take a good picture if you don't know how to use it."

"That sounds logical. My mom taught me to cook and I went to culinary school but most of my knowledge comes from trial and error," I tell her.

"Yeah," she smiles at me in agreement. "I had to take classes and learn the technical aspects of working my camera but I also had to just play and break the rules and figure out what worked for me." Finally finding a scent she likes, she holds it out for me to smell.

"It reminds me of you," I say, and then regret it.

She sets it back down and walks further down the table. I'm afraid I've made her uncomfortable, even though I hadn't meant to. "Liv..."

"Shush for a minute," she whispers and I'm too shocked to continue.

Did she really just "shush" me? What the hell?

She lowers herself down to her knees in front of one of the cloth-covered tables and pulls her camera out of the bag. I notice her making a few adjustments to knobs on the top of the camera and turning a dial on the back near the large screen. Liv then points the short, stubby lens toward a long row of hand dipped candles and I hear a rapid clicking as she takes several pictures.

"Okay, you have my permission to speak again," she tells me with a triumphant smile.

"Your permission?"

"Yeah. If you plan on being my assistant today, you have to shut the fuck up when I find my shot."

I can't help it. I start to laugh. *Where did this girl come from?*

For the next hour, I find myself playing tour guide, enjoying the laughter and smartass comments and being completely fascinated by Liv at work. She avoided the obvious things that I, in my amateur ignorance, thought would make a nice photograph. She would instead focus on seemingly random and mundane things that were unexpected. Now, I find myself getting more and more excited to see the final results. I can't remember the last time I enjoyed a day more.

Eventually, we come to one of my favorite stalls for fruits and I remember I need to grab the things Sabrina had asked for. Liv is checking out large wire baskets filled with bright red cherries.

"Oh, that's right. You mentioned loving cherries. Would you like some?" I ask as I inspect the small containers of fresh black-berries and raspberries.

"Oh, fuck!" Liv sputters and my head whips up and over in her direction. I'm aware of the gasp of a nearby elderly lady, in her Sunday best, checking out the baskets of peaches. What could be wrong?

"Liv?" I reach a hand out for her, confused by the sudden look of panic in her eyes, as she backs away with quick, small steps. She might have made a successful escape if she hadn't backed right into several stacked crates of large, ripe honeydews and cantaloupes and fallen backward into them.

"Holy sweet shit on Sunday!" Profanities are her specialty.

A gentleman would have run over to lift her back onto her feet but I continue to stand where I am. I'm choking on laughter, as her ass plants itself deeply into one of the half depleted crates, forcing her feet up into the air. She's throwing the fruit out of her lap and flailing about in desperation, yet still I do nothing. *I'm such an asshole.*

"You're such an asshole!" she yells at me.

Our shared opinion just makes me laugh harder.

"Liv? Is that you?" a tentative, male voice from behind me

interrupts my enjoyment at her expense.

She groans and rolls her eyes upward. "No, Freddie, I'm a figment of your imagination so move along. Nothing to see here!"

The guy she called Freddie snorts, steps forward, and helps her out of the crate. I just stand there like a moron, feeling helpless and irritated. *Who is this guy?*

Average height and build, he's pale and freckled with blonde hair and thick-framed glasses but not bad looking. He also looks completely enamored of my photographer.

"Daddy! Daddy!" A chorus of high, childish voices precedes a little mob of blonde heads as four... no, wait *five* kids circle Liv and the stranger.

"Hey, squirts!" This time, Liv's face shows only open joy as she ruffles hair and doles out one-armed hugs.

"Whatcha holding, Wiv?" asks one of the younger girls. She's cute with long braids, pink cheeks, freckles, and a missing front tooth.

The innocent question causes all of us to look at Liv. One forearm is supporting two large cantaloupes against her chest, victims of her recent assault to their crate obviously, but it's apparent she'd forgotten all about them.

"Oh! Ummm..." She furrows her brow slightly. "These are my melons, Cassie."

Immediately, Liv's creamy skin flushes a deep pink as she realizes what she said and I'm in awe as this brash, tough woman, queen of the biting one-liner, is completely flustered by a child.

"And they're such nice melons too," the man whispers loudly. *I would very much like to beat the shit out of him.*

"Hilarious, Freddie," Liv deadpans as she drops the melons into a basket behind her and apologizes to the stall owner.

"Liv?" I feel like an intruder. The two of them have completely forgotten about me and it bothers me more than it should.

"Oh, shit!" she turns to me but then quickly pivots back to the kids to apologize. "Ugh! Sorry, squirts! Don't listen to me. Never repeat the things I say, okay?"

"Okay, Wiv," they intone in unison.

"Zac," she gestures toward the man and continues, "this is Freddie."

I don't like him but I put a hand forward and smile anyway. He doesn't look as though he likes me either but he takes my proffered hand, squeezes firmly and pumps it a couple of times.

"I'm here with Zac to take some pictures for his new restaurant. It's a work thing," Liv explains.

Freddie's face lightens with relief. "Great!" He sounds a little too pleased in my opinion. "That's great. The kids and I were just getting out and enjoying this weather. They go stir crazy if we stay indoors too long."

"Well it's nice to see them again," she says while bending down to talk with each one of them in turn.

She's really good with this guy's children. Are they close? Do they spend a lot of time together?

"It's really nice seeing you again, Liv," Freddie tells her and I'm tired of feeling like I'm invisible.

"So, Freddie," I say loudly, to draw their attention, "it was great to meet you but maybe we should..." I raise an eyebrow at Liv and she takes the hint.

"Yeah," she adds. "Sorry, but I need to finish this up."

"Of course," he grants. "But maybe later..."

"Maybe," Liv interrupts quickly, "but I'm so fuc... uh, I mean, I'm so crazy busy right now." I feel a little tingle pulse through my arm when she grabs my elbow and starts to steer us away from the mini herd of blondes.

"I'll tell Kelly hello for you!" she calls over her shoulder as she waves and takes long steps that have me shocked her short legs and high heels can even manage.

Allowing myself to be pulled along, I steal a glance behind me, and Freddie is watching us walk away.   He should be noticing that one of his toddlers is disappearing under a cart with large buckets filled with flowers.

"So, Freddie is..." I let the implied question dangle but she ignores me. "And five kids?" I add, trying again to get her to share. I'm dying to know what the story is between them.

Liv halts so abruptly I almost crash into her backside. Lips pursed into a tight line, arms now crossed below her chest and creating, even more, cleavage, she cocks a single eyebrow at me in reprimand.

"None of my business?" I guess. It really is none of my business and I should just leave it alone but my curiosity is killing me.

Sighing heavily, she relents. "He's just a guy I went out with a couple of times. You met Scott and Kelly at the engagement party, right? They set me up with him."

I think about when I had been introduced to Logan's college buddy Scott and his wife. Kelly had been a little bundle of energy and smiles and I'd liked them both instantly. They know Liv a lot better than I do but had they really thought this guy was a good match for her?

"Well, Freddie seems to like you," I admit. What I really want to tell her is that I don't think he's right for her at all. She can do much better. *I'm such an ass. I don't even know the guy. Maybe he's perfect for her.*

"He's nice," she concedes.

"And he's got five kids?" *Who even decides to reproduce that many times in this day and age?*

"Obviously," she smirks.

"Is that why it didn't work out?" I need to let go of these personal questions but for now, she seems willing to answer and I want to know.

She starts to smile. "Who says it didn't work out?" We both know she was practically sprinting to escape him from setting up a future date. "It wasn't the kids. I mean, it was a little shocking when I first found out but I actually had more fun spending time with them than I did with him."

I laugh and she winces. "Well that made me sound like a bitch," she admits. "Freddie is a fine man. He just wasn't the one for me. You know?"

I take a step closer and look down into her sincere face and bright green eyes. The corners of her full lips turn up slightly and she lays one small hand on my arm. I stop breathing.

"You know what I want?" she asks.

"What?" My voice cracks and she's so close now I can smell her perfume. It smells like gardenias and honeysuckle and makes me think of lazy summers spent outdoors.

"I want what you have." This confession is simple and direct and I can't think of one damn thing to say. "I want real love. I want a marriage of shared dreams, friendship, and overwhelming passion. I want what you and Sabrina have."

All teasing and lightness have left. "You'll find it, Liv. You deserve it." I take her camera bag from her and turn toward the exit. "I think we've had enough for today."

Chapter Five: Liv
Girls Only...No Boys Allowed

"You aren't putting that in my bar!"

"It's temporary!" I promise with a wink as I grab hold of his giant bicep, spin him around, and try to maneuver my boss back into his office. Since he is a solid block of stubborn muscle, I don't get far.

"I didn't agree to this, Liv!"

"You said we could have Charli's bachelorette party here, Ronan. Why go bar hopping, when we work in a bar?" This is a completely logical argument in my opinion. He should quit giving me so much grief over it. *Doesn't he trust me?*

Ronan closes his eyes, takes a deep breath, and runs his open hand down his face, from forehead to chin, before trying to reason with me again. "I thought you meant some alcohol and playing pool. That's what we did before I got married." This must be stressing him out because he never mentions his failed marriage, normally.

"Well, we will definitely consume some alcohol. We might play some pool... but since Charli vetoed my plans for a male stripper..."

"So you decided *becoming* strippers yourselves was a good idea?" Poor guy. His face is an angry red, his scowl lines would now classify as canyons and he's starting to hyperventilate.

"We won't be stripping. Well... at least, I don't *think* we're stripping. The brochure didn't say anything about actually removing clothing."

Ronan is no longer red, he's now almost purple and he sinks down onto the nearest barstool.

Coming into the bar, carrying several stacked cases of beer, Kyle stops in concern. "Ronan? Dude, are you having a stroke? Maybe you should lie down."

"He's fine, Kyle." I say confidently, but honestly, he does look pretty bad. *Should I worry?* "He's just a little surprised by my plans for Charli's bachelorette party."

Kyle looks between Ronan and I and starts to grin. His smile is amazing. Actually, he's pretty amazing even without the smile.

Kyle is the bartender at Ronan's bar, The Crash, and Charli and I both waitresses, but we have some big plans in progress. I love all of them like family, not that I would admit it of course. Giving my coworkers a regular helping of sarcastic shit is more my style. I also live in the apartment above the bar. It is also owned by Ronan, so it's a good thing I don't hate him. I still can't believe Charli moved out to live with Logan. I know they are getting married but we've lived together since she lost her parents at thirteen. Also, I'm not good at the "Suzie Homemaker" shit and she kept the place from ending up on an episode of Hoarders.

"Did you hire a male stripper?" Kyle asks, with a look of disgust. "Because if you did, I understand Ronan's objection. Why would he want some guy stripping down and rubbing his junk all over his bar?" He shudders at the thought.

"No! I did not hire a stripper! Damn!" *Do they listen to me at all?*

"Well, what the hell is that thing?" Kyle points to the stage area near the back of the bar, where a sweaty guy in a wife beater and with four inches of exposed butt crack, is installing a gleaming chrome pole.

"It's temporary!" I hiss. He doesn't look convinced.

"But, what is it for?" Kyle insists.

"I hired this company that comes out and teaches women how to pole dance. It's supposed to be a great workout and lots of fun."

"Is that guy the teacher?" he asks, and now I'm the one shuddering with disgust.

"Of course not! He's just setting up the pole. The instructor is a hot blonde with porn star tits." She's also very good at what she does but I know that isn't the type of detail Kyle cares about.

A wicked grin slides across his face and his dark eyes twinkle. "So, this hot blonde is going to teach you, Charli, and all your hot friends how to strip on that pole? Count me in!"

"Oh, for fuck's sake! We won't be stripping! Didn't you hear that part?"

"I just heard the hot, tits, and pole."

"Of course, you did." I shove him and he laughs.

Kyle is unbelievably hot, with long dark hair, mischievous eyes, and all kinds of bad boy swagger. Once upon a time, he had a thing for Charli but luckily he'd gotten over it and they have remained friends. *It's a shame we didn't fall for each other since I love him to death, but he's more like a brother and that would be fucking gross.*

"It's a moot point anyway," I tell him, "because you aren't invited. It's girls only. So take Ronan with you and be gone by seven, please. The guests should arrive by eight."

"But, Liv..." he gives me his sexy "come hither" look but it doesn't work on me.

"No!" I point toward the door and he finally relents.

"You're a harsh bitch sometimes, babe."

"I know." I plant a quick kiss on his cheek and head over to check on the pole progress.

Chapter Six: Liv

You Bitches Are Vile

"Oh my God! Oh my God! Oh my God!"

"Shut up, Charli! It's going to be fine!"

"Liv, Ronan is going to kill us!" I can tell Charli's panic is about to hit the point of no return.

"We will just fix it before he comes in tomorrow. He'll never know." I try to reassure her but I'm having a hard time even convincing myself.

Ronan is a tough, ex-military badass and he runs his bar like a tight ship. No nonsense is allowed and everyone has to pull their own weight. Thank God he loves Charli and I like daughters, even though he pretends we drive him crazy.

Okay, we probably do drive him crazy, but he still loves us.

"Really? Who will be able to fix this in the middle of the night? We're totally screwed, Liv." Charli's voice has gone up, at least, an octave and if she doesn't calm down soon, I'm going to have to find a paper bag for her to breathe into.

"What about Logan?" I ask. "Can we call him?" He'd already had his night out with the boys last weekend so he should be home in their apartment now. He might not be excited about being woke up at two in the morning but tough shit.

"What can Logan do? He's a great lawyer but he's not a handyman. I had to hang up the pictures you gave us because when he tried, he busted his thumb with the hammer!"

"Shit. We're screwed."

Charli's bachelorette party had started out perfect. Kelly, married to Logan's friend Scott, had arrived first.

"Yay! I see Jello shots!" Kelly had yelled as soon as she set down her platter of penis-shaped cookies on the bar.

"Kyle helped me make a new drink for tonight too. He's calling it 'slut punch' and it's very fruity so Charli will love it," I told her.

Kelly walked over and gave Charli a tight hug. She loves hugging. It's not my thing but to each their own. "Charli, I know this is your night," she told her, "but I need this so bad! The twins are driving me insane. It's good for Scott to have to deal with them on his own for a change. He has no idea what my days are like while he is away at the office."

Charli laughed sympathetically. "I'll bet he put you on speed dial for tonight."

"I'm turning my phone off!" Kelly had said and proceeded to do just that just as Brooke and Chelsea had arrived. They both waitress with Charli and I and are always up for a party.

Sabrina had been the last to show up, but she was well worth the wait. She had contributed several trays of finger foods and snacks that Zac had prepared.

"Damn! No wonder you work out so much," I told her. "I'd

never be able to pull away from the table with food like this all time."

She laughed. "Yeah, Zac is amazing in the kitchen. He even remembered to make some snacks that Charli will like since this is her celebration." We all make fun of my best friend's eating habits. Charli lives on fast food and crap.

With the liquor helping to lower our inhibitions, we'd all been ready for our pole lesson. Music pumping, we changed into some little gym shorts and tank tops and wrapped feather boas around our necks. It had been explained to us that we needed some exposed skin to be able to grip the pole properly. Basically, slutty clothes are a safety precaution.

Our instructor was great. She explained and demonstrated before expecting us to attempt anything. Everything looked like it was shaping up to be a great night.

Halfway into the evening, I leaned in close to Charli and whispered, "Ummm...I'm beginning to suspect Brooke and Chelsea moonlight at the strip club two blocks over."

"Liv!" she scolded, but she couldn't help laughing.

"Those bitches are *too* good!" I'd insisted.

Sabrina, in such good physical condition from her job, hadn't taken long to master most of the moves either. Charli is tiny and thin but not very limber and her spastic gyrations had provided a lot of comic relief. I'd had some trouble with some of the maneuvers because of my big boobs but I wasn't horrible.

How in the hell do all those skanks with giant fake tatas end up exotic dancers?

And then it was Kelly's turn. "I got this, bitches!" she yelled after slurping down another Jello shot. She's average sized and in good shape, especially considering she carried and delivered twins less than two years ago.

How does a body ever recover from that shit?

She might have had way too many Jello shots, in retrospect. Kelly got the motion down quickly and started feeling pretty confident. In fact, she was confident enough to let go with one hand and twirl her boa while screaming, "woo hoo." This loss of fifty percent of her grip was enough to send her careening off the pole backward into the shelving unit that Ronan had custom designed to hold the bar's stereo equipment.

The shelves became dislodged and spilled black boxes and wires all over the floor. When Kelly tried to get up, she became twisted in those wires and reached out for support. Since we were all standing there in shock, with our mouths hanging open and offering no help, she grabbed onto the lower cabinet door and ended up pulling it completely off the hinges.

Yep, we're screwed.

And now, Charli and I stand together, in shared horror. We're looking at the disaster of wood, wires, and technology and wondering how many years Ronan will be reminding us of how untrustworthy we are. When Kelly joins us a few minutes later, she's still pretty unstable and Charli puts an arm around her waist to lessen the chance of another catastrophe.

"I'm sho...ummm... I mean, I'm SO sorry. I don't know what happened!" Kelly whines while using both hands to support her own head.

"Jello shots," I tell her. "Jello shots happened."

"Are you mad at me, Liv?" She looks ready to cry, or maybe vomit, or maybe cry and vomit.

"Of course, she isn't. It was an accident," Charli reassures and gives her a tight hug. Then Charli takes a step back and looks in my direction to encourage me to agree. That's not happening.

"How's Scott with tools?" I ask her. I'm not optimistic. We've been friends for over a year now and I don't recall ever hearing about him fixing anything. He's probably as bad as Logan.

When I decide to fall in love, he better be good with his hands. I mean, for obvious reasons of course, but being handy around the house is important too.

"Oh, he is so good with his tool!" Kelly giggles and even tries to wink. She just looks like some demented owl with her mouth open and both eyes opening wide and closing together. I groan. She's still so intoxicated.

"His tool gave me twins!" she adds too loudly. She thinks this is so funny and she now has tears running down her face.

"Focus, Kelly!" I grab her shoulders and shake lightly. "Could he fix this?"

Her laughter stops, and she looks really pale. "Ummm... Nope. He's not good at that kind of stuff. I had to put together the girls' toy box. And did I tell you about the swing set they got for Christmas? It was a tragic loss."

"Damn," I say while still holding onto her shoulders. Then, I notice she's beginning to go an odd shade of green. "Kelly?"

"Sorry!" is all I hear before copious amounts of vile red vomit, with little Jello chunks, completely covers my brand new pair of silver stilettos. It takes all I have not to add to the mess when I feel the warmth seep between my toes.

"Oh, Liv," Charli whispers, "Ronan is going to kill us."

"Charli," I whisper back, between clenched teeth, "right now I'd like to be killed."

"Ewwww," Sabrina contributes while gagging and pinching her nose to hold back the stench. She's just joined us but I can tell she is rethinking that decision.

"Thanks. That's very helpful," I throw back. The puke is cooling quickly and it's gluing my toes together. I close my eyes and count to ten while breathing through my mouth only.

"I could call Zac," Sabrina offers. At least, I think that's what she's saying. Her voice is so distorted from the closed off nostrils, I can't be entirely sure.

Charli suddenly looks hopeful. "Could he fix this?"

"Maybe. His dad taught him woodworking and he's built a lot of the stuff at the restaurant."

"Call him!" Charli begs and Sabrina heads off to find her phone. Maybe she's just trying to escape the smell of my vomit covered feet.

Charli grabs paper towels and garbage bags from behind the bar but takes one look at the floor and pales.

"I just can't, Liv. I love you but..."

"Ugh! You're a pussy. Just take Kelly to the back and help her clean up."

I don't need to tell them twice. Charli grabs Kelly's arm and they haul ass for the back storage room with the tiny utility sink near where we store the mop and broom.

I open the first garbage bag and, using paper towels, I slip my defiled shoes off and throw them away. They'd cost me almost two hundred dollars but no amount of money in the world could make me try to clean them now. I then use two more bags to wrap both of my bare feet so they look like they are wearing giant, foot condoms. I hold my breath as I wipe up as much as I can off the floor. Then, sliding across the bar floor in a skiing motion, careful to make sure my filthy feet stay wrapped, I make it to the ladies' restroom. I crawl up onto the counter and stick both feet into the sink basin in order to clean them off completely. I have to stop twice to close my eyes and fight the urge to throw up.

By the time I feel clean enough to crawl out of the sink and strong enough to stop gagging, I step out and see Kyle is mopping up the rest of the crime scene. He's also shaking his head in disgust.

"Thanks," I say. "When did you show up?"

"Charli called me and I came over to help. You bitches are vile."

"I'm not even going to disagree with you."

"Scott just picked up Kelly too and I think I heard Logan a minute ago."

"Good. What about Brooke and Chelsea? And the instructor?"

"Those girls are pros at partying. They didn't even blink an eye... just called a cab and split. You know they don't want to be here if Ronan figures this shit out and shows up." I nod my head in agreement. "And the hot teacher left and said she'd send someone for the pole in the morning. She kept muttering about needing a new job."

I sit down on a barstool and lay my head down on my arms in defeat. Kyle finishes the cleanup, pats my back consolingly and then leaves to take the mop bucket out. I enjoy a few minutes of solitude.

"Wow. Sabrina said it was quite a party, but... Wow."

My head jerks up at the sound of his voice. I need his help but damn it's embarrassing that he's here to witness the aftermath of this debacle.

Hey, Zac," I stutter slightly, "Thanks for trying to help. Sorry, it's so late." I feel awful about him having to get out of bed at this hour just to help me out. I'm sure it's for Charli's sake since he and Logan are friends. After all, I'm just his photographer.

"I don't mind," he says and comes closer to me but I flinch away. He looks hurt.

"Sorry," I tell him, "I reek. I'd stay away if I were you."

"Oh," he says and his body relaxes. "I understand."

"I'm glad someone understands because I'm at a total loss right now." I sigh heavily and close my eyes in frustration but keep talking. Once I open the gates, I can't seem to shut up. "My brand new shoes are ruined. I liked those shoes. I love all my shoes. And Ronan is going to kill me, and I deserve it. He trusted me with his bar! And I stink so bad I want to vomit myself. And..."

I feel something warm and wet slide down my face.
My eyes jerk open in shock and I slide my hand along my cheek. "Shit! And now I'm fucking crying! I don't cry, Zac!" I tell him forcefully. I hate to appear weak.

He laughs lightly, as though I'm being ridiculous. *I guess I am.*

"I'll never tell," he promises and I feel better.

"Oh, Zac! Honey, I'm so glad you're here." Sabrina rushes over and into his arms. He wraps her in a tight hug, but remembers my predicament and manages to turn her so that her back is to me and I have enough time to dry my face.

"I'm here. Show me this disaster." He's talking to her but looking at me.

Sabrina leads him over to the destroyed cabinet and I watch as he frowns and inspects the damage. It looks bad and I'm trying not to get my hopes up.

"I can do this," he decides, and I let out the breath I hadn't realized I was holding.

"Really?" I ask.

"Sure. I just need to grab my tools out of the truck."

"I can do it," Sabrina offers. She gives him a quick peck on the cheek and heads out the back door, to the parking lot.

"If you manage to pull this off, you have my undying gratitude," I tell him. And I mean it.

He laughs and he winks at me. "Anything for a damsel in distress."

"So, you're my knight in shining armor?" I ask sarcastically, but smiling so he knows I'm teasing.

He smiles back for a moment but then his face falls and he is looking at me very seriously. It makes me nervous.

Has he taken my comments wrong? Does he think I'm flirting with him? Oh God, am I flirting with him?

He takes a deep breath. "Liv…"

"Hey," I interrupt, scared of what he might say, "would you mind if I run upstairs to my apartment and get a real shower? I hate to leave you with this mess but…"

He stands there without saying anything for several seconds. His eyes are locked onto mine and I can't look away. "No, it's fine. I've got it," he finally says. His voice is strained and even though he said I can go, I don't want to.

He leans toward me and I know it must be to pat my shoulder in sympathy or something equally innocent, but I'm so flustered by my own behavior, that I jump back a little. He looks away from me and I see him swallow hard. If I'd let him actually touch me, my shower would have needed to be a really cold one.

Chapter Seven: Zac

Lady, Your Hair is VERY, VERY Red

"Thank you again for fixing the cabinet. You can't even tell it was ever damaged." Liv leans close to whisper this into my ear, close enough for the warmth of her breath to tickle and the smell of gardenias to flood my senses.

I'm careful not to move my head when I reply. She's facing me and near enough that a slight turn would bring our lips dangerously close. That would be extremely awkward and also highly inappropriate with my fiancé only a few tables away.

Shit, my thought should have been that it would be highly inappropriate, regardless of where my fiancé happens to be.

"You're very welcome. I'm glad I could help you out," I tell her.

I was happy to fix it for her. She looked so upset and all I wanted to do was make it better. Liv's fun to be around and her conversations are teasing and keep me on my toes... but they also make me forget who I am sometimes and the fact that I'm engaged to someone else.

I'd almost ruined everything that night at the bar, right before she'd gone up to take a shower. I had been dangerously close to reaching out and moving a stray curl from her face. I'd watched it in fascination as we spoke and I'd longed to see if it was as silky as it looked.

Surely this is only pre-wedding jitters, right? Please God, let this just be my nerves.

Liv smiles and raises her champagne glass to me, before taking a small sip and looking back toward the bride and groom. Her nose twitches from the bubbles and I can't resist smiling back. She looks incredible tonight.

The bridesmaid dresses Charli had chosen are a deep charcoal gray, strapless, and short. With Liv's red hair pinned up, but still loose and soft, the startling contrast to the dress has been drawing the gaze of every guest at the reception. I don't think I've ever seen her look more beautiful.

Charli is breathtaking too in her white satin gown that's simple but elegant. It shows off her tiny little frame and the thick dark hair perfectly. Logan, in his traditional black tux, is practically glowing with pride. He looks so damn happy.

I hope that on my upcoming wedding day, my happiness shows as plainly.

The reception venue is small, intimate and overlooks a large garden. A separate table had been assigned, near the newlywed's table, for the wedding party. So here I sit with Scott, Logan's sister Jenna, and Liv while Sabrina sits at a table with my parents and little brother. I keep looking over to make sure she's okay but she seems fine as she laughs at my dad and whispers with my mom. I'm sure they're talking about the wedding. It's all they do lately.

I haven't seen her talk to Mikey once. I know she loves my brother but his handicap makes her nervous. She gets so flustered sometimes that I think she decides it's easier to just avoid him.

When people start to migrate toward the dance floor, I'm finally able to join my family. Arriving at their table, I notice Sabrina has drifted off near the bar.

"Mom, Dad," I reach down to hug them both. Their tight returning grip reminds me how hard my move away from my hometown had been on us all.

"It was a beautiful wedding," Mom says. "I can't believe yours is so close." She lifts her napkin and dabs at the corner of her eye.

"Well, it's about time!" Dad adds. "You guys have been together for ages and I'm ready for grandkids."

"James!" Mom nudges his shoulder. "I told you not to pressure them!"

"We aren't getting any younger, Ginger."

"It's okay, Mom," I say to stop her from getting onto my dad again. "I'm looking forward to starting a family soon too."

"Oh!" she beams with excitement. "I'm so glad! I know Sabrina has always been...well, reluctant... to talk about babies."

I cringe. I hadn't realized my parents had picked up on that. "She isn't ready yet and we haven't even said our vows," I remind them, "but we've talked and agreed we won't wait too much longer."

"Good. Good." My dad says with a big smile but I notice my mom's face has a slight frown.

I leave my parents' side of the table and walk around to where my little brother, Michael, sits. His arms are drawn slightly in and his head is moving to the music as he smiles at all the dancers.

"Hey, Mikey!" I kneel down, so we are eye to eye, and I see

the recognition light up his sweet face.

"Zac!" He throws his long gangly arms around me and pounds on my back with both fists.

"Are you having fun?" I ask him. I know Mom had a hard time getting him to wear his suit instead of one of his superhero T-shirts but he looks great. He's such a handsome young man.

"Yes, Zac. It's fun. And they have cookies. And Mom gave me cookies. I really like cookies."

"I know you do. Logan remembered how much you like cookies too, so he made sure they had them here for you, buddy."

"I like Logan. He got married today and he has a wife now. And she is really little. She is littler than me. Because I'm big."

He's so proud of being big. And he really is. He and I had both inherited our height from our dad and even though he's only fourteen now, I'll bet he hits near my 6'4" by the time he's an adult.

"Zac?" Her voice is soft, almost a whisper, but I'd know it anywhere. It feels wrong that's it's so familiar to me.

I turn away from Michael and for the first time, thanks to my kneeling position, I'm looking up instead of down into her delicate face.

"Who is that, Zac?" Mikey pulls on my sleeve insistently. "Who is lady with red hair? Lady, your hair is very, very red."

"Mikey," I admonish. I'm sure Liv will understand but sometimes his observations make people uncomfortable.

Liv, with no hesitation, places her hand on my shoulder and stops me. "He's fine, Zac. Please introduce us."

I smile at her and then at Mikey. "Liv, this is my little brother, Michael."

"No!" he screams at me. "I'm not little! Mikey is big now."

Liv grabs the nearest chair, pulls it close to his and sits down.

"You're right, Michael. You are a very big guy. Much bigger than me!"

"Yes. Much, much bigger than you, red hair lady."

"You can call me Liv if you want to."

"Yes, I can call you Liv. You can call me Mikey. It's better than Michael. You are very, very pretty, red hair Liv."

She smiles and reaches out to take his hand into hers. She does it slow and carefully, in case he doesn't want her touch, but he slides his long-fingered hand right into hers and smiles.

"I like red," he whispers loudly, and even Mom and Dad smile over at us. "My fire trucks are red."

"I like red too, Mikey," she shares and just like that, she's won his heart.

After meeting my parents, listening to them go on and on about the engagement photos she'd taken for us, and saying goodbye to Mikey, I walk beside her to the bar where our friends are hanging out.

"Thanks," I say before we've covered the full distance.

"For what?" She looks genuinely puzzled and it fills me with a surge of affection that she doesn't realize her simple acceptance of my brother is something special.

"For talking to Mikey and being so patient with him." Frowning, I think of how often he's ignored by people that assume he's not aware enough to notice.

Liv smiles up at me and loops her arm through mine as we walk. Even as short as she is, it's a good fit and feels comfortable. No, maybe comfortable isn't the right word. It feels *right* and that's a very uncomfortable thought.

"No thanks necessary," she assures. "I loved him. He's a great kid."

"He really is. I wish others could see it. He was born with a chromosomal disorder and mentally will probably never progress beyond the developmental age of four or five but he's loving and kind..." I reach over and tweak the tip of her nose, "and he possesses amazing instincts about people."

"There you are!" Sabrina comes over and takes my other arm. "I saw you introducing Liv to your folks." She leans forward, to look past me and talk directly to Liv. "They loved the photos as much as we did! I'm so glad Charli and Logan's wedding gave you the opportunity to meet both of them before our big wedding day."

"They're great," Liv agrees. "And I already love Mikey. He's so funny and sweet. I'll bet he is getting super excited about his big brother getting married and gaining a sister."

"Oh," Sabrina falters. "I guess I didn't think of it like that." She laughs. "Some of the things he comes up with are pretty funny."

"Do you have siblings?" Liv asks Sabrina.

"I have one older brother but we aren't very close. I do expect him at our wedding, though. My parents are divorced and have both remarried. There are lots of aunts, uncles, and cousins too, so I will have lots of family for you to photograph. I haven't seen some of them in ages."

"That's great. My family is small so I'm always a little envious of people with larger families. Not that I'm complaining of course. My moms are great and I have Charli."

Liv looks happy and untroubled and it's nice that her family is so important to her. Sabrina smiles and I get the impression she's unsure what to say.

"Well," Liv says, breaking the silence, "I'll leave you two to finally enjoy some time together." She takes her arm out of mine and smiles one last time. "Zac, I loved meeting your parents and brother. They're great. I see that my moms are hanging out with

Charli, Logan, and his folks, so I'm going to join them." She gives a little wave in farewell.

Sabrina and I continue to walk toward the bar, but once Liv is a good distance away, she leans closer to me and whispers, "I was so shocked when I realized Liv's parents are lesbians. I mean, it doesn't bother me or anything but I'm surprised Logan didn't warn us."

I stop and Sabrina falters. "Warn us?" I ask.

"Well, yeah. I didn't know what was going on when two women walked Charli down the aisle until Kelly explained it to me later. I knew Charli had lost her mom and dad when she was young and then she had been raised by Liv's family but no one told me that meant two moms."

"I don't think most people feel the need to warn others about their family situation. I don't run around telling everyone I meet that I have a handicapped brother. All families are different and you just have to accept there's no such thing as normal."

"Okay, I'm sorry. I didn't mean to offend you, Zac."

"I know." I sigh and give her a quick kiss. "You didn't. I don't know why that came out so pissy. Sorry."

"I love you, Zac."

"I love you, too."

Chapter Eight: Liv
Define Okay

"That's good but let your hand just drop down behind you and look off toward that big oak tree. I don't want you looking directly at the camera this time and remember to put your weight on the back foot," I tell her and she makes the changes I ask for. "Perfect."

Adjusting my aperture for a really shallow depth of field, I snap a few more shots before walking over to where Sabrina stands. Her dress is the purest white, a mermaid silhouette, and although it's strapless, she's added a lace bolero to give it sleeves. The cathedral length veil is edged with matching lace and her dark hair has been pinned up to showcase the graceful column of her long neck.

"You look beautiful," I tell her. "There aren't a lot of women that can do justice to this style of dress but you're so tall and thin, it's perfect."

"Thank you, Liv!" She smiles radiantly and looks even more beautiful. "We are having the ceremony in church so I wanted traditional but I liked that I can remove the sleeves for the reception at the restaurant.

"Great idea. When is Verde' opening?" I like that I will be photographing their reception in such a beautiful venue.

"Zac swears everything will be complete by the wedding but the grand opening will be the weekend after we return from our honeymoon."

"Sounds like you two have everything worked out." I pull the topmost layer of the veil over her face and gently nudge her chin toward the diminishing sunlight. "Just let me get a couple more close-up shots and we can call your bridal session a wrap."

I like the pensive, slightly tensed expression on her face, it's very editorial and wicked cool, but it's not reading "happy bride-to-be." I doubt her family and friends will appreciate the high art look of it as much as I do. They'll want to see joy and excitement.

"Sabrina?" I lower my camera and step closer.

"Hmmm?" She continues to stare off at the horizon and hasn't even noticed I've stopped shooting.

"Is everything okay?"

"Define okay."

Shit. This doesn't sound good. I know I shouldn't get involved and it's none of my business. I've been so careful to keep my distance from Zac for the last couple of months. When we did end up at the same place at the same time, I tried to make sure we were never alone.

It's just too hard to remember he's taken.

The best thing I can do is stay as far out of his personal life as I can, but she looks so troubled. She's actually close to tears. *How am I supposed to ignore that?*

I can't. I like her.

"You want to talk about it?" I pray she doesn't. *Please let her tell me that she's just fine and there's nothing to talk about!*

"I'm scared, Liv," she confides quietly.

"It's just cold feet," I assure her. "It's totally normal. Every bride goes through it."

I've never been married, but this is what they say, right? I've heard this can be a normal reaction right before a wedding, even though I would have thought you would be excited when you're sure of the guy. Charli hadn't had any doubts about marrying Logan and Sabrina and Zac have been living together for a long time. So, what's going to change in her day to day life, other than her last name and the status on her income tax forms?

But maybe I'm being naïve. Making a vow before God to love, honor, and cherish one person for the rest of your life shouldn't be taken lightly. I try to smile sympathetically.

"I've loved Zac since we were practically kids," she explains. "I don't doubt my love for him or his for me."

"Good! Then you have no reason to be scared."

"But, marriage is different than love. What if we can't make it work? Do you know the statistics for divorce?" Her voice starts to take on an edge of panic.

"That's because most people are dumbasses," I say and she snorts with laughter. "Zac is an amazing guy, mostly because he understands how amazing you are. He doesn't take you for granted. And, like you said, you love each other."

"But there are things that..." She looks away and I wonder if she'll continue. I want to help her and listen if she needs me to, but... *If she starts telling me personal shit I shouldn't know, then I'm out.*

"Sabrina, maybe..."

"I just don't think I can handle kids!" She blurts, facing me now, and her expression is full of defiance.

Damn, I didn't tell her she had to procreate!

"Okay. I take that to mean Zac does want kids?" I ask.

"YES! It's so important to him. He said we don't have to start a family right away but he doesn't want to wait too long and he wants, at least, two. I just don't think I will be a good mother."

"I think everyone worries about that. I'm sure one day my spawn will terrorize everyone they know and be aware of every foul word in the English language. But they'll know I love them. Your kids will have that too."

"And what about Michael?" she whispers.

"What about Mikey?" I try to keep my voice calm but a small fury is bubbling up.

Is she afraid of having a child like Zac's brother? We all want our children to have the best and I get that he deals with some hardships because of his condition but he is wonderful and loving and such a special young man.

"Zac's parents won't be around forever and one day it will fall to us to take care of Michael. You know Zac would never put him in a home or something."

"Of course not!" I yell and she winces.

"I didn't mean that he should! But I don't know if I would be the right person to take care of him. He deserves better than me."

My anger dissipates with this admission. I shouldn't have assumed the worst. "Oh Sabrina, don't sell yourself short. All that boy needs is love and you will be fine. You won't be alone. Zac will be there at your side. He would never expect you to shoulder it on your own. And I'll bet, after you've enjoyed some time as a married couple, you'll want to make a little person that comes from the love the two of you share."

She bends down to compensate for our height difference, wraps her arms around me, and locks me into a fierce hug. It's a good thing I like her because I'm usually not down for the touchy-feely thing.

"Thank you," she snuffles into my hair. It's kind of gross and I try patting her shoulder in hopes that it hurries up this emotional crap so I can step away.

"Sure," I comfort, "Ummm... about your bridal shoot..."

She laughs and lets me go. "I know they will be gorgeous. Thank you, Liv. Thanks for everything."

Chapter Nine: Liv

Is it Wrong?

I pull my best friend out of her chair and drag her off to the ladies' room. Logan furrows his brow but keeps his seat. He's used to me hauling Charli away when I need her. They've been married for a couple months now but she's been my best friend for my whole life.

"What's wrong?" she asks as soon as the door swings shut behind us.

I bend down and look under each stall door to make sure we are alone and then crumple onto the bench in the small sitting area that adjoins the bathroom. "Charli, be honest with me. Is it wrong to be at a wedding and want to fuck the groom?"

"Oh, Liv..." Charli lowers herself beside me and pulls my head over to rest on her shoulder. "I was afraid of this."

I jerk my head up in shock. "What do you mean, you were afraid of this?" I yell. "You knew and didn't say anything?" I'm practically shrieking now.

"Shut up! Someone is going to hear you! In case you forgot, there is a wedding reception taking place out there and I doubt you want Zac and Sabrina's family and friends to realize you're hot for him!" Only Charli can yell at me in a whispered voice and sound so serious.

"If you suspected, why didn't you tell me?"

"If you felt like this, why didn't you tell me?

"Good point. I was embarrassed," I admit.

"You're never embarrassed," she counters.

"Okay, well maybe not embarrassed... but ashamed. I don't play with things that aren't mine. I really like Zac. Yes, he's amazing to look at but he's also fun to be around. He gets my sense of humor, which probably means he's a little off, and he isn't intimidated by me, either. He loves his restaurant and what he does, he adores his brother, and he loves..."

"He loves Sabrina," Charli finishes.

I bury my face in my hands and groan in frustration. "I know."

"Do you?"

"Yes, damn it. I do. And I can't even wish that he didn't love her because then he'd be a douchebag for stringing her along. I want him but if he wanted me too, then that would be awful. I don't want him to doubt his love for her and I certainly couldn't want someone that is capable of cheating. I'm completely screwed."

"Yep, pretty much." She wraps an arm around my shoulders. "But I still love you. And I know the right guy is out there and when you find him, this won't even matter anymore. In the meantime, I'm sorry."

"I can't even get drunk. I still have to take the rest of the damn wedding pictures."

Charli's commiserating laughter fills the small room and echoes off the marble. When the door opens and Zac's mom walks in, I thank God we aren't still discussing my lust for her son. I got the impression she liked me when we met at Charli and Logan's wedding but knowing I want to do naughty things to Zac might alter her opinion.

"Hello, girls," she says as she walks over to us.

"Hey, Mrs. Reynolds. Good to see you again. How are you?" I ask. *Smile and act like you aren't dying a little on the inside, Liv. You can do this.*

"Please call me Ginger," she insists. "Olivia honey, Mikey is asking for you. He usually needs time to warm up to people but he took to you immediately. I couldn't tell you the last time he was so excited by someone new. Would you mind terribly stopping by the table to talk to him again? I hate to impose. I know you're busy but he just won't give up asking for you."

"Of course! I'd love to. I'll go now." I jump up and head for the door and as it swings shut behind me, I can hear her telling Charli how wonderful I am. Charli is nice enough not to mention all my faults and instead agrees with her.

Walking over to Mikey's table, I can't help but look for Zac on the way. He and Logan are near the cake table, drinks in hand, and laughing at something one of them has said. His eyes catch mine and he raises his glass slightly in my direction but I quickly look away and pretend I didn't see him.

"Hey, Mikey!" I sit down in the chair next to his and a smile instantly covers his precious face.

"Hey, Liv!"

"Having a good time?"

"It's okay. Want to know a secret?" he asks as he leans in a little closer.

"Absolutely," I whisper, back.

He reaches up and pulls on the knot in his tie. Slipping it over his head, he then undoes the top two buttons of his dress shirt and opens it to reveal the Superman shirt underneath.

"I'm Superman!" he tells me. "But Mom says that when he goes around people, he wears his disguise so no one knows. It's called a secret idenemy. You won't tell anyone about my secret will you?"

"Never! Your secret *identity* is safe with me." I crook my little finger toward him, take his hand and bend his finger in a similar fashion and then show him how to "pinky swear."

"So, that means we have to always, always keep our secrets, right Liv?" His earnest face melts my heart. He has no reason to hide his feelings or thoughts. I envy him that freedom.

"Absolutely. You can tell me anything," I promise.

He leans forward again but before he can confide anything else, his eyes look past me and he smiles over my right shoulder. "Zac!" Mikey yells excitedly and I tense.

"Hey, buddy. What evil plans are you two hatching over here?" Zac asks as he joins us.

"It's a secret. A very, very important secret and I can't tell you. And Liv won't tell you either." Mikey looks at me with a mischievous grin. "Will you, Liv? You promised you won't tell my secret, remember? Remember the pinky promise, Liv?"

"I remember," I assure him. "I won't tell."

Mikey wraps his thin arms around me and I reciprocate by wrapping mine tightly around him. For the first time, I have no personal space concerns at all. I adore this kid.

Within seconds, Mikey has pulled away from me and is looking at his big brother in challenge. "I'm going to get some cake. Mom says I can have cake because I ate all my weird food you made, Zac."

"Weird food?" Zac puts his hand to heart. "You wound me, buddy!"

"I didn't wound you! I don't even have my new lightsaber with me. Mom said I couldn't bring it." He crosses his arms and scowls as Zac and I both try to hide smiles at his obvious indignation.

Mikey almost immediately forgets the wrong against him though and jumps up to run toward the dessert table. "Bring me a piece of cake too!" I call in his direction before he can get too far away.

"Okay," he yells back over his shoulder. "I'll bring you a big, big piece. You are small and you need to get big like me."

"I could love him just for saying that alone!" I admit with a smile. "I know I'm short, but I'm not tiny like Charli, so it's awesome to be thought of as small." My words aren't meant as a complaint. I'll never be model thin or able to wear all the clothing styles that my best friend can pull off flawlessly but I have no problem with my curves. I've learned to play them up and own them.

"Liv, you *are* small," Zac says softly, as he slides into the chair that his brother just vacated across from me. "My hands could span your waist. If you mean that you are shaped like a woman instead of a stick, then believe me when I tell you that's an asset. Any man," he pauses to look me over slowly, "would consider you perfect just the way you are."

My breathing becomes shallow and my mouth opens slightly as my cheeks start to flush. I feel like I need to say something, to joke away his words like I normally would, but there's a tightness in my throat and my brain has gone into shutdown mode. *I need to get up and leave. I need to run.*

"Zac..." I start, but I can't think of anything to say. This is his wedding. There's nothing I can say. *He isn't stupid. He has to see how flustered I am and how ridiculous I'm acting. Why isn't he running from me?*

"So, you have a secret?" he asks softly.

My heart thunders in my chest. *Holy shit. He does know. He's figured out how insanely bad I want him.*

"Wh-what?" I stammer.

"Mikey said you two have a secret?" He leans even closer and I can smell his warm spicy cologne, the tang of the alcohol he's just consumed, and even that green herbal scent he always carries on his hands from his hours in the kitchen.

"Oh..." I exhale softly, relaxing a little as I realize he was just asking me about Mikey and not my secret desire to climb onto his lap and shock his wedding guests. *Okay, that might be a bit of an exaggeration. I'm not into the whole "public sex" thing. I'd, at least, pull him into his office or something before taking advantage of him.*

We continue to sit across from one another, our faces only inches apart, for what feels like an eternity and still not nearly long enough. He's staring at my mouth and my lips feel suddenly so dry. I want to lick them, moisturize the poor things, but I'm frozen by his stare.

Then, without warning, he jerks back away from me like I have the Bubonic Plague. He stands up so abruptly the chair goes skittering backward and a few guests at the next table look over at us in surprise.

"I uh..." He looks around in desperation and swallows hard. "I need to go find Sabrina."

I look up at him in silence until he finally stills and looks back at me. "Yes, Zac. You do."

Chapter Ten: Liv
What Have We Done?

I don't want to do this. I don't want to be here. Please God, let Sabrina be here.

"Hello?" Walking into the quiet, dark restaurant, I'm struck by how different it is this evening. Zac and Sabrina's wedding reception had been here only a couple of weeks ago at this same time of day but then lights and candles had blazed and lit every corner of the room. Now, with my eyes still adjusting from the brightness of the vestibule, all I can see are the stars and nearly full moon through the large windows.

Why is it so dark in here? They knew I was coming.

"Sabrina?" My voice echoes with a loudness I hadn't antici-pated. I feel like I've stepped onto the set of a B-grade horror film. Any minute now, the masked serial killer will slide out of a dark corner to kill me in some gruesome way that involves more blood than a human body even contains. *After all, only the virgins survive those movies, right?*

"She isn't here." His voice is low, deep and gravelly... and it nearly scares the shit out of me. I stumble and reach for the nearest chair to steady myself.

"Zac?" I whisper reluctantly. Logically I know it must be him but I've never heard him sound like this and I'm still a little spooked.

"Yeah, just me," he says and I finally pinpoint a location. If I strain my eyes, I can just make out his silhouette at the bar, backlit from the ambiance lighting on the liquor shelves.

"Where's Sabrina?" I ask nervously. *She told me she would be here!*

"She's working late."

"Okay, well..." I need to just turn around and leave. *Maybe I can ask Charli to take care of this for me tomorrow?*

"Come have a seat, Liv." It sounds like a command and I don't respond well to being told what to do.

"I don't think so. I'm just here to drop off the prints, so I'll go now."

"Please, Liv," he begs and my heart squeezes tightly in my chest. Instead of a gruff demand, his second request sounds pitiful and lonely.

My heels make loud, steady taps as I cross the cavernous room. I'm relieved when I finally make it to the stool next to his and there is silence once again. He doesn't acknowledge that I'm next to him, but he has to be aware. My skin prickles lightly from his nearness and I wait to see what he'll say.

He just continues staring forward, at the shelves of alcohol, taking small sips from the glass of amber liquid in front of him.

"Zac..."

"Wedding photos?" he interrupts.

"What?"

"Are you here to drop off the wedding photos?" His voice is calm and without expression.

"Oh...ummm...no. I've brought the final, framed prints for the restaurant. I left them stacked against the hostess stand for you. The wedding prints should be ready in a couple more weeks."

"Okay. Thanks."

There is still no emotion in his voice and it's freaking me out. He's usually smiling and easy to talk to and besides, he just got back from his honeymoon so he should be on a sex high at least.

Has something happened with his restaurant? Is his family okay? "Zac, maybe I should just go..."

"Don't go, Liv. Please. I don't have a right to ask but I just need a friend right now."

I'm not the person he should be talking to if he's having a problem. I'm no one to him. I'll just leave and call Logan on the way home and give him a heads up. They've been friends for a long time and he'd make a much better confidant.

"I really shouldn't..." I say even though I feel awful about it.

"Please." His voice breaks during his plea and I'm undone. Even knowing I should leave, I can't. This is the first man I've ever known that I can't walk away from.

"Okay," I relent, and I see his shoulders sag with relief. *He really expected me to say no. If I had half a brain, I would have said no!*

We sit in silence for several minutes. I decide it's up to him if he wants to talk or just have another human being near for comfort.

"Our honeymoon was great," he says finally, and even though his words were spoken so softly I barely heard them, they seem to swell around us. "We had two weeks of relaxation and fun and just enjoyed being together."

"I'm glad." I try to wait patiently for him to continue and explain what has him so dark and still.

"And then we came home and back to our real lives. I work all day at my restaurant, my grand opening is only a couple of days away, and she spends all day at the gym making sure they understand what a team player she is," he says this like he's reciting a grocery list.

"Reality is always harder than the time we spend away from the day to day grind. You know that," I tell him.

"I know," he laughs with no humor. "The work hours don't cause any problems actually, but I do miss her of course. And tonight we finally managed to have dinner together. It was nice. After dessert, I asked her if we could please talk about our future, about maybe buying a house and planning a family. We've discussed this before. It's nothing new but in the past, she's always said she wasn't ready quite yet and as soon as we got married we would make our plans. She always said soon. Soon."

"Just give her time. You've only been married a couple of weeks," I remind him.

"I know, but we've been together for ten years now and this was always our plan. I'm not trying to rush her. I swear that I'm not. If she needs more time, that's fine. But tonight, when all I wanted was to start saving for a down payment on a future house... so we would be ready when we do decide to...well..." he takes a large gulp and finishes off the drink. "Tonight she said she's pretty sure she never wants kids." He lays his head down on his crossed arms, resting on the bar in front of him like the world has dealt him a blow he can't withstand.

I tentatively place my hand on his shoulder, knowing physical contact is dangerous, but unable to help myself. "Don't give up on her. She loves you. She's just scared. It's a big decision."

Raising his gaze to mine, the anguish I see breaks my heart. "What if no amount of time changes things?"

He is still staring right at me, and I want to tell him that she will change her mind and everything will be fine. But I can't know that.

"Some people are naturals with kids," he continues. "Some people are nurturing and giving and..." He stops midsentence and I wonder if he's afraid to say more. It probably feels like he's betraying her just by admitting his worry.

"Let me get you a drink," he says abruptly, and without waiting for my response, he jumps up from the stool and is behind the bar.

"Oh, no. That's okay. I'm good."

But he has already pulled out a glass and fills it halfway from a crystal decanter. Alcohol, an intimate atmosphere, and my secret lust aren't a healthy combination. It's past time for me to leave. I tell myself to just go...now.

But...maybe a quick drink will help me deal with this clusterfuck? I'll just have one, to make him feel better. So just this one, and then I'll go. I won't make any more excuses.

We drink in silent companionship for a long while. The only sounds are the ice cubes rattling against the glasses as we lift and lower our drinks and his intermittent sighs. I'm enjoying the way the alcohol is warming my center and I can feel my muscles relaxing. The decanter doesn't have a label and I'm not sure what it is... but I like it.

"Sorry you had to catch me like this," he says, breaking the silence. "I'm not usually so depressing."

"We all have our moments but don't make a habit of it," I tell him with a wink and a raised finger for emphasis. "I'm not cut out to be the one who saves the day."

"Oh," he glances over at me, "I think you are."

"Hmmm," I have to look away. To keep myself occupied, I concentrate on running my finger around the rim of my glass. This makes him notice the glass is now empty and he grabs the decanter to refill it.

"I can't," I protest. "I have to drive home."

"I'll call a cab. No one likes to drink alone." He's not open to arguments.

"Okay." *Fuck it.* This shit is good and it's the first time that horrible knot in my belly has loosened enough to be bearable. I accept my full glass and take another sip.

"Tell me about your family?" he asks, as we settle in. "I need a distraction."

"Well, you've met my family. Dana and Carol are my moms and they're great. They run the Garrett Charity Foundation, although Momma D handled most of it while I was growing up and Mom stayed home with me. After Charli's parents died when we were thirteen, she came to live with us, so she's more like my sister."

"I really liked your moms when I met them at Logan and Charli's wedding."

"I liked your family too," I tell him.

"Thanks. I'm grateful we're so close. I was so excited when I found out I was getting a little brother. My friends thought it was weird that I was already a teenager and my parents decided to have another baby but I didn't care. I loved him from the moment I first saw him. When we realized about his handicap, I was devastated. It was so unfair and I lashed out at everyone."

"I'm sure they understood."

69

"My parents are amazing and they forgave every stupid ass mistake I made, other people weren't as forgiving."

"What happened?" I ask.

"When Mikey was about four, and I was eighteen, I'd taken him to a playground near our house. There were only a few kids there at the time and he wanted so badly to play with them. They were close to his age and accepting of him, like a lot of really young people are, but there was this guy that caused a scene. He was seventeen and the older brother of one of the younger kids there. He told his little brother to stop playing with the *retard* and I lost it."

"Oh, Zac..." I die a little on the inside, imagining how horrible it must have been for him.

"So I hit him. He was close to my size and not about to let it go, so he hit back. He had his keys clutched in his hand and he pushed one between his index and middle finger so it stuck out. He went for my eye. I realized what he was doing at the last second and ducked enough it ended up hitting a little high. It split open my eyebrow and crushed a small piece of my upper eye socket."

"I wondered how you got the scar," I admit.

"Yeah, I'm not proud of it." He looks down at his glass and swirls the remaining ice cubes around.

"Maybe you should be! That guy was an asshole and it's a good thing I wasn't there or I'd have probably shot him!"

He laughs. "Logan told me you're quite the sharpshooter. He said you love going to the gun range and your aim is scary good. He also warned me to never challenge you to a game of darts."

"I'm just getting ready for the zombie apocalypse. You can't blame a girl for being prepared," I say, and he laughs again. It's nice to see him finally relaxing a little. "So, what happened after the guy hit back?"

"Someone had called the cops, and head wounds bleed a lot, so I looked pretty bad. The kid got scared and ran off but we lived in a small town and everyone knew who he was. My parents were pissed and disappointed but decided to let it go. His parents didn't feel the same."

"Really? He almost took your eye out!"

"Yeah, but he was technically a minor and I was an adult. And I hit first. It cost my parents quite a bit to resolve it and I still feel guilty about that."

"I'm sorry." I don't know what else to say.

"It was a long time ago."

"I know but I'm still sorry you had to go through that."

"Liv...," he says, but then stops and looks away.

"What, Zac?"

"It's just so easy to talk to you." His voice isn't quite slurred but it's no longer precise either. *How many drinks had he had before I showed up?*

"Really? I think most people find me abrasive and hard to deal with," I confess and he laughs again.

"Well, your language is very colorful at times but you're refreshingly honest."

"Honesty can hurt," I admit and I'm sure he hears my warning.

"It can... but you aren't cruel. You point out the obvious, with humor and kindness."

His body leans closer to me and I can feel the heat of him as he reaches forward. With the back of his hand, he caresses the side of my cheek and my eyes close involuntarily.

"And Mikey loves you. I always trust his opinion of people," he whispers and I open my eyes to see his face is only inches

71

away.

Our alcohol-scented breath mingles and I'm paralyzed. My cheek is burning from his touch, my brain is in a fog from too much booze, and my breathing is doing this funny, hitching thing.

"I love Mikey," I whisper.

His pupils are so large in the darkness that there is only the thinnest ring of warm chocolate around them. I watch as his gaze moves down from my eyes to my lips. I swallow hard and dart my tongue out to moisten them. He leans even closer, slow enough to be asking permission, and my brain is telling me to run but my body won't listen. Instead, of its own accord, it leans to meet him.

His lips feather against mine so softly I barely feel them. Then I hear him moan from deep in his chest and his arms are pulling me up tight against him. The sensation of his mouth pressed against mine, his tongue insisting on entrance, and the heat generated from our body contact is beyond anything I've ever experienced. I'm so lost in him, I can't tell where I am or what I'm doing.

And then he pushes me away in disgust and I fall back to reality.

"Oh, God," he closes his eyes, as though the sight of me sickens him. "What have we done? What have I done?" He leaves me standing alone at the bar and paces the length of the dining room.

"I'm sorry," I choke out.

"No!" he yells and strides forcefully back to me. Grabbing me by my shoulders, he lightly shakes me. "This isn't your fault! It's mine! I'm the one that's married. I was feeling sorry for myself and had too much to drink."

"I shouldn't have..." I'm trying to apologize but an apology is useless.

I know better. This is my fault. I've wanted him since I first saw him and as soon as he needed a friend, I let things go too far. I'd known he was in a vulnerable state and I hate myself for allowing this.

"Liv! Listen to me! You didn't do anything. You're so damn beautiful and I've been attracted to you from the start. I was hurt by the things Sabrina said but I should never have taken advantage of your kindness."

I snort. He's a fool if he thinks he took advantage of my kindness. I gave in to my lust. *It won't happen again.*

"I need to go." I walk toward the exit.

"I'll call a cab for you but wait in here with me."

"No," I insist. "I'll call for my own cab. And I'd rather wait outside."

I can't stand the pain on his face but I know it's for the best. I will make sure we are never alone again.

Obviously, I can't be trusted.

Chapter Eleven: Liv
The Really Far Away

"Hello?" I hear her answer the phone and my stomach feels sour with dread. *Did he tell her?* And even if he didn't, I know what I did and the guilt is eating me alive. It has been three weeks since that night at the restaurant... the night I kissed *her* husband.

"Hey Sabrina, it's Liv." *Is my voice giving away my nervousness?*

"Hey! I've been waiting to hear from you!" Her excitement is clear, so obviously she doesn't know I'm a lying, cheating whore and I took advantage of the man she married.

"Sorry, it took so long. There were so many images to edit that it takes more time for wedding photos than my regular sessions," I explain. I've actually had the images ready for over a week but it has taken me this long to grow the balls to call her.

"I completely understand, I'm just so anxious to see them.

Are you bringing them by Verde'?"

I had foreseen this complication and no way in hell am I stepping into that restaurant again. I'm not ready to see Zac either, so I have a plan. "Actually, I was hoping you could run by here and pick them up? I'm having some car issues so it would be hard for me to drop them off."

"Oh, okay. That shouldn't be much of a problem but I have to work pretty late tonight so I'll just ask Zac to run over and -"

"No!" I yell into the phone. *For fuck's sake, Liv. I'm sure Sabrina won't think it's at all weird that you just interrupted her to scream that you don't want her husband to come see you.*

Trying to sound nonchalant, even though that ship has sailed, I say, "I mean, sure he can if that's easiest for you... but it doesn't matter to me if you come late. I'm working tonight too and it's a bar. We're open until two in the morning. I can take a break when you get here and we can talk a little. I'll even buy you a drink."

"That sounds great. See you tonight!"

She hangs up and I just sit there, staring at the dark screen, scared at how fucked up my life is right now.

"Liv?"

I look up to Charli, standing in my living room, waiting for me to respond. "Hey. How did you get in here?"

"I knocked but when you didn't answer, I tried the door. You know, you really should lock it."

"Well if I locked it, then how would my nosy best friend invade my pity party?" I ask.

Coming over, she curls up next to me on the overstuffed couch we used to share. Logan hated it and refused to let her take it to their apartment when she moved out, so 'win' for me. Looking at me, she patiently waits for me to explain. Well, patiently at first

75

but after several minutes, she punches my arm and commands me to spill.

"Your best friend is a home wrecking whore," I admit.

Her eyes bug out and her mouth drops open. Very little that I do shocks her anymore, so now it's even more apparent how awful my actions were. "Did you sleep with him?" she whispers.

Why is she whispering? Who does she think is going to hear her? It's just us in my apartment.

"No, thankfully even cheating hookers like me have some limits." I see her visibly relax with this revelation.

"What happened?"

"I went by to drop off the pictures for the restaurant and he and Sabrina had been having an argument. He was alone and drinking and feeling sorry for himself... so of course, I got drunk with him. Then...we kissed."

"You kissed him?" she asks, as though she's trying out the notion to see if it's plausible. I know her well enough to realize she's working hard not to judge me, and I appreciate that, but I deserve her disgust.

"Well," I think back to the night I've been trying desperately to forget, "actually, he kissed me... but I didn't stop him."

"He kissed you!" The shock has returned to her face.

"Damn, am I that hideous? You don't have to act like I'm a troll and it's impossible for someone to want me!"

"I didn't mean that at all and you know it. I'm just surprised. I knew how you felt about him but I don't know Zac well enough to guess at his feelings and I really thought he loved Sabrina."

"He does! He does love her! He was just drunk and made a mistake." I bury my face in my hands.

"He doesn't seem the cheating type. Logan always talks about how great he is and how good he and Sabrina are together.

I'm just wondering if he feels something for you too. Why else would he risk what he has?"

"He doesn't feel anything for me." I look directly into her face, sure of my words. "I told you, it was just a mistake. He realized it almost immediately and pushed me away."

"Oh," Charli looks at me with pity and again I feel the acid in my stomach churn. "I'm so sorry," she says.

"Don't be! I deserve it and more."

"Stop it. I'm not saying it was right but you obviously both regret it, so just let it go and never ever let it happen again."

"It won't. I can promise you that. In fact, I've made a decision that will guarantee it."

Warily, she asks, "What decision?"

"A couple of weeks ago Momma D called and told me about a job opportunity. I've been seriously considering it but it has some complications. Now that I've created my own complications here, it's looking better and better."

Charli narrows her eyes. "Exactly what kind of complications does this job entail?"

"A lot of traveling. It would be an eighteen-month photography assignment that would have me hitting up more than a dozen different countries."

"You are leaving me for a year and a half?" she screeches, and I wince. My poor eardrums actually ache.

"You know we live in the technical age, right? Cell phones and email are a part of daily life so we'll keep in touch." I'm a little apprehensive about being away from everyone I know and love for so long too, but I know this is the right decision.

Charli doesn't look happy. "What about the bar? Ronan will be pissed." She crosses her arms over her chest and nods her head once, as though she's found a plausible excuse for me to stay.

"He'll understand and I'll help him find someone to replace me before I go. You'll be here to help train the new hire, so it's not a big problem."

"What about the apartment?" she throws out, trying again. She's starting to look desperate.

"I've actually thought about that too, and I have an idea."

Ronan gives me a hell of a deal on my apartment and I love it. The industrial style loft with huge windows is ideal for my photography business. Charli loves this place too and I know she prefers it to the apartment she and Logan are in now.

"You were just saying that your lease is almost up, and it's too expensive for you and Logan to really save for a house while staying there. I know you were planning on finding a cheaper place, so I was hoping you two would move in here. The rent is low enough for you to really work on that down payment you need. And then I can keep all my crap here still, so it's a win-win."

"Really?" I can tell she sees the merit of my plan and is excited by the possibilities. She had been sad to leave this place and I would have been okay with Logan moving in here when they got married but the thought of all that newlywed sex, and our thin walls, had been a little revolting.

"I need this, Charli," I assure. I don't want her to feel any guilt about being excited over getting the apartment back.

"I'm going to miss you so badly, though." She leans forward to hug me but I playfully push her away.

"Of course, you will. I'm an awesome bitch and no other friend can take my place."

"I have one condition, though," she tells me and I see the spark of mischief in her eyes.

"What?"

"When I give birth, you have to swear you'll come home."

"You're knocked up?" Now I'm the one screaming while she laughs.

"No, not yet but we've decided not to wait any longer. We want to start our family now, so when it's time, I need you here." She looks happy but she's serious. I know it's important.

"Absolutely. Nothing could keep me away." This time, I let her hug me.

After exhausting our imaginations for cool baby names - *I still think Winchester is a kick-ass suggestion* - she feels the need to hug me one last time and wipe her tears on the hem of my shirt before leaving.

I am going to miss her so much. Am I sure this is the right decision?

Knowing I don't have long before starting my shift at the bar, I'm about to head off to change clothes when my phone rings. The screen shows a number I don't recognize and I'm apprehensive, but I accept the call. It could always be a new photography client.

"Hello?" I say in my most professional tone.

"Liv? Is this Liv? This is Mikey and Mom said I could call you."

I break out into a smile at the sound of his sweet voice. "Hi, Mikey. How are you?"

"I'm good. I'm playing Legos today. I built lots of cool stuff. Want to come see it?" he asks.

"I'd love to but you don't live very close to me, remember? It would take too long to get there and I have to go to work tonight."

"I know. Zac told me that."

Just hearing his name hurts. "Can you send me a picture of what you built? Does your Mom let you text pictures? Or can she help you?"

"Yes! She helps me do that. I can do that."

"That would be great. I would love to see it," I tell him.

"Can you come see me, Liv?" he begs and I want to get in my car and drive the two hours it takes to get to his house.

"I can't, remember? It's too far and I have to go work."

"I know that, silly! But we are going to visit Zac. Mommy says we will go in fourteen days, just like I am fourteen now. Mommy got your number from Zac so I could call you and invite you to visit me when I come to visit Zac. Will you come see me and Zac?"

The last thing I need to do is see Zac again, but I would love to spend some time with Mikey. *How do I explain to him that by next month I won't even be here anymore?* "Mikey, I would love that but I can't. I'm so sorry!"

"Why? Why can't you come see me and Zac?" He sounds like he wants to cry and I feel my throat tightening.

"I do want to come see you! I really do! But I have a new job and I have to leave soon. I'm going to be really far away."

"Can I come visit you at the really far away?"

"I think your Mom and Dad would just miss you too much because it would take you a long time to get there."

"Can I call you at the really far away?"

"Yes! Mikey, I would love for you to call me. You can call me anytime you want and if your Mom helps, you can send me pictures and I'll send you pictures of all the neat places I'm going."

Thank God for cell phones. I will miss Charli and Logan and my moms and my friends... and this special little guy that has taken over my heart so quickly... but at least, we can stay in touch.

"Okay, Liv. I will miss you but send me pictures of the really far away."

"I will, Mikey. I promise."

Chapter Twelve
Snail Mail Sucks

(Two Months Gone)

Charli;

Hey, hooker… miss me yet?? I've given up trying to call you this week because my phone reception here sucks. Instead, you get an email
update, which isn't as good as getting to hear
my voice, but better than snail mail any day
of the week. And besides, those international
phone plans are too damn expensive.

Hope you and your husband (God that's weird to
type) are enjoying the awesomeness of my kick
ass apartment. I'm sure you two are going at
it hot and heavy in an attempt to make a little
human, but STAY OFF MY COUCH, OUT OF MY ROOM,

AND AWAY FROM ALL KITCHEN SURFACES (because that is just damn unhygienic).

How is the new waitress working out? What's her name again? Madelyn? Marilyn? Has Ronan made her cry? Has she tried to jump Kyle? We already know both will happen, if they haven't already.

I am attaching some photos I took this week, here on Ko Samui. The beaches in Thailand are unreal. The sand looks like sugar, the water is clear and aquamarine, and the groves of palm trees make all my pictures look like they belong in a travel guide to paradise. I would say you'd love it, except you'd probably starve to death finding something you'd actually eat.

Tomorrow I'm going on a tour on the back of an elephant. I know I'm not exactly an "animal" person, but I'd be lying if I said I wasn't excited. And this bitch doesn't lie.

I think next week I'm leaving here for Mumbai. I'll keep you posted.

Miss you more than I'm comfortable admitting, hooker!
Pregnant yet????
-Liv

Liv,

Thailand?! That's so far away! I miss you so
much but I'm excited that you are getting to
have this adventure. And the pictures you sent
were AMAZING! One day you will settle down and
try to make little humans too, so it's great
that you can do this now. Selfishly, I still
wish you were here with me, though.

We aren't pregnant yet. I'm trying not to get
discouraged. It's only been a couple of months
and I know stress makes it harder to conceive.
Kelly wants me to go with her this weekend for
a massage and spa day. I love her and appreciate that she wants to help me relax, but let's
be honest, we both know she probably wants a
day away from her twins too. Those beautiful girls just turned two and they are little
monsters!

The new waitress, as I've told you THREE times
now, is named Madison. Ronan has made her cry
twice but she's tougher than she looks and has
stuck it out. I can tell he respects that and
is finally warming up a little. She probably
can't tell the difference but with time, she
will figure out what a softie he really is.
She did spend the first week staring in awe at
our Kyle, no surprise, but didn't try anything
because she has a boyfriend that she's crazy
about. The boyfriend is a lucky man because

resisting the temptation of Kyle isn't easy. He sends his best, by the way. Which of course means he said, "tell that beautiful bitch I love her and can't wait for her to get her ass back here where it belongs." Ronan just scowls and leaves the room when your name gets brought up. He'll never fess up to how much he misses you but we all know.

You didn't ask, and I don't know if you want to know, but we've seen Zac and Sabrina a few times since you left. They seem to be good, so whatever problems they were having must have blown over. His restaurant has become THE place to eat here in the city and even the food critics have raved about it. I know you'll be glad for his success. Sabrina was promoted at her job too and she's the assistant manager of the gym now.

I know you are keeping in close contact with your moms but I wanted to let you know that Carol and Dana have invited Logan and me over for dinner next weekend. I'm really looking forward to it but it won't be quite the same without you. They are so incredibly proud of you and so am I.

Better run, it's almost time for my shift.
Love and miss you;
-Charli

(Three Months Gone)

Olivia;

Hello, this is Ginger Reynolds - Mikey and Zac's mother - and I hope it is okay that I am writing you. I asked Zac to get your email address from Logan because Mikey wanted me to send you a picture he drew for you and I don't know if I can send pictures internationally with my phone plan. I took a photo of his drawing and will add it to the end. Again, I hope this was okay, but my little guy can't quit talking about you and you were so wonderful to him at the wedding. You are a very special young woman.

This is the message Mikey asked me to type, directly from him:

Liv, this is Mikey. I miss you. I will draw you lots of pictures for when you come home and come see me. I love playdough and I made a lady with the red playdough on her head to be her hair and be like you. Love from Mikey. Come home.

I hope you are having a wonderful time seeing the world and look forward to seeing your photographs when you are back if you don't mind sharing them with us.

Thanks again;

-Ginger

(Three Months, Three Days Gone)

Ginger,
Thank you for sending Mikey's picture. I love
it. I saved it to my phone and look at it often. Please continue to send new ones, anytime
he draws them, and I love to hear his messages.
I will definitely come to see you when I'm home
again and I'd be honored to show you my photographs.
-Liv

P.S. Tell Mikey, I miss him and I bought him
a surprise gift for when we finally see each
other again!

(Six Months, One Week, Two Days Gone)

Liv,

Hey. I'm not sure what to say or if I should even be writing this. Probably not. I've attempted this letter more times than I care to admit over the last few months but I'm determined to actually send it this time.

I'm so sorry about what happened. It was my fault. Please tell me you didn't leave because of what I did. I don't think I will ever forgive myself.

I think about that night often. Mostly it's with guilt but sometimes with something else that I can't explain. It's probably best if I don't even try.

I hope that one day you can forgive me.

You are one of the most amazing women I've ever met.

-Zac

(Seven Months, One Week Gone)

Liv,
Well, you never answered my last email, so I guess it's safe to assume you don't want to talk to me. I won't bother you again.
-Zac

Charli,

I fucking miss you. I miss the bar and Ronan and Kyle. I miss my moms. I miss Zac. What the hell was I thinking when I decided to go halfway around the damn world? Are you knocked up yet?

-Liv

(Twelve Months, Three Weeks, One Day Gone)

Charli,
Email sucks!!!!! I hate that you can't "un-send" shit you decided to send when you were drunk!
Please completely disregard last night's email. I was feeling sorry for myself and got totally wasted in a rowdy little pub in Inverness last night. I mean, I do of course miss all of you. Well, almost all of you. Please pretend I never said that I missed HIM. It was the Glenfiddich talking. That damn fine whiskey also landed me in a game of truth or dare with some brawny Highlanders and I now know what the Scots wear under their kilts…not a DAMN thing! But I do still want to know if you are knocked up yet?
From your very hungover and headachey (that should totally be a real word!) friend,
-Liv

(Twelve Months, Three Weeks, Two Days Gone)

Liv,

Your two emails made me want to cry, freak out in panic, laugh until I wet myself, and most of all, jump on a plane to find you.

I do hope your headache is better. Stay away from the whiskey and those Scots. And just how much did you see under this brawny Highlander's kilt? Did you have sex with him??? And more importantly, since you're in the area, did you get some pictures of that Loch Ness Monster?

I know you don't want to hear about HIM - but he did tell Logan he tried to email you and you won't respond. Maybe you should. I think there are some things you guys should work out. Since you have asked, the answer is no. I'm not pregnant. We've been trying for a year now and I'm beginning to worry it will never happen. We have an appointment with a specialist next week. I'll let you know what happens.

Love and miss you so much!

-Charli

Charli;

It WILL happen. And you will be a fucking amazing mom. Never doubt it!

I love you and I expect an immediate email after your doctor's appointment.

I cannot believe I've been gone for more than a year already.

Didn't see old Nessie, major disappointment, but tomorrow I leave for Ireland and it's an isle known for magic so who knows what adventure will find me next.

Love,

-Liv

P.S. Please, let's not talk about him anymore. It's ancient history.

P.S.S. NO! I did not screw the Highlander. I just got a good look at his assets as he proved his "truth" by flashing the whole pub.

Liv,

The doctor ran some tests and he has some ideas
about why I'm not conceiving. It has something to do with my ovulation, the eggs aren't
maturing properly, so they started me on some
medicine to help with that. I also have to
give myself hormone shots once a month when my
ovulation begins. It sucks. And I'm a weepy
mess. I think I'm driving Logan crazy. Maybe
you're lucky to be so far away right now. I'm
trying to stay positive but it's so damn hard.
The next four months need to hurry up. I need
you, Liv.
-Charli

Charli;

Only one more week until I'll be home! I talked to my moms last night and they guilted me so hard for being gone this long. Did Momma D forget she was the one that found me this job and encouraged me to go?

I'm in Brussels now, but I leave for London day after tomorrow and it's my last stop on this whirlwind trip. Are you and Logan still able to get me from the airport?

Tell Ronan, Kyle, Scott, Kelly and the whole gang I expect them all to be waiting at the bar to see me when I get there too. I have gifts for everyone and I'm worth the wait.

I know you were disappointed again this month but I still haven't given up on your uterus. It's a tough bitch, just like you, and I know it's capable of giving me a little niece or nephew to corrupt into awesomeness.

See you in seven days, ten hours, and fourteen minutes.

I love you, hooker.

-Liv

Chapter Thirteen: Liv

Deliver Me From Evil

I splash some water on my face with total disregard for my makeup and pray the medicine kicks in soon. If I arrive home looking like Patient Zero for the zombie apocalypse, no one will believe my world travels had actually been a good decision.

The doctor here in London had been kind enough to prescribe antibiotics, a nasal spray, and a thick, disgusting cough syrup that also promises drowsiness.

Please let the cough syrup knock me out enough to sleep through the whole transatlantic flight!

Stuck on a plane between two complete strangers, trying to be polite when they invariably offer small talk, is not appealing. I can tell the meds are finally helping though, so hopefully this nasty sinus infection will be history soon.

After my last bathroom break on foreign soil, I make my way to the gate. The screen mounted near the information desk as-

96

sures me the flight is on time and I'll be boarding soon, so I locate a chair in the waiting area as far away from the other future passengers as possible and sink down to wait.

I scroll through my phone and read over some of the recent texts and emails from Charli. She's trying so hard to sound positive but I feel her desperation. You always assume that when you decide to start a family, you will be able to enjoy lots of unprotected sex and make a baby easily because that's what our bodies are meant to do. *Even undeserving and unprepared people pop out kids regularly, so why should you encounter any difficulties when you're young, healthy, and ready?*

But my best friend has a doctor's appointment almost every week, takes daily medication, injects herself in the stomach monthly, and cries herself to sleep every twenty-eight days. It's killing me knowing there isn't a damn thing I can do to make it better.

Next, I flip through my collection of pictures from Mikey. Ginger had been nice enough to email them to me over the months I'd been gone and they never fail to make me smile. She'd also promised they've been saving the originals in a big red folder, per Mikey's request, for when I'm home. I'd honestly expected him to forget about me with so much time elapsing since our last real visit. The fact that he hadn't forgotten puts a golf ball-sized lump in my throat and threatens a bout of tears every time I dwell on it too long.

And now, despite knowing better, I give in to the temptation that I'd sworn I was over. *You have to stop this, Olivia.*

I do this at least once a week though in the beginning it had been multiple times a day. Considering today is the day I go home, the day I take myself back to the same city he's in and back to the friends we share, I'm lucky I've managed to hold off this long.

The edges are curled and torn and the picture is looking dirty and abused after eighteen months of travel and repeat viewings. But even if it fades to nothing, its image is burned into my mind and locked into my memory. It has become a part of me.

The loud, abrasive voice coming through the speaker system announces, in multiple languages, that my flight is now boarding. Stuffing my reminder of what I can't have back into the front pocket of my backpack, I hoist it up over my shoulder and head for my gate.

Herded unceremoniously through barrier ropes, temporary tunnels and rounded metal doors with air locks, I finally make it down the narrow aisle to locate my seat. I'm happy that's it next to the window, I won't feel as claustrophobic, but groan realizing it will mean a lot of "excuse me's" every time I have to squeeze past my neighbors to get to the bathroom.

I open the window's sliding shade, slip my bag under my seat, and fasten my safety belt. Within minutes, a heavy-set man in his forties squeezes into the seat next to me. I've been on more flights than I care to recall over the past year and a half and I really want to know why I never get to sit next to the person in need a few extra pounds. I always get the ones that love a buffet line a little too much.

Damn. I'm a bitch. I hope my piss poor attitude is the result of my cold or the grogginess setting in from the prescriptions meant to relieve it.

He's probably a great guy and I have no room to judge. After all, I'm the horrible person that kissed a married man.

Even though a lot of time has passed and I've had so many experiences, good and bad, I still can't shake my guilt. In order to atone for my ungenerous thoughts toward my in-flight neighbor,

I turn my head and smile at him.

He takes that as an invitation and smiles back. "Hi, beautiful. I'm Greg." He shoves a meaty hand in my direction.

Shit. What have I done? "It's nice to meet you," I say politely and shake his hand as quickly and as lightly as I can, before making a point of turning toward the window.

"Come here often?" His baritone laugh booms and several nearby passengers look over in annoyance. They, like me, are probably very concerned about his proximity for the next several hours.

I give him the smallest and most insincere laugh I'm capable of, and again turn away.

"But really," he continues, undeterred by my lack of interest, "do you fly often?"

God, save me. "Occasionally," I respond curtly, praying for him to get the hint and let it go.

"Well, I fly a lot on business. I own my own company." He says this with great pride, so again I smile weakly, even though I'm dying to tell him to leave me the hell alone.

"But I'll tell you," he says as he leans too close, "this is the first time I've had the pleasure of getting to sit next to someone as sexy as you."

Deliver me from evil, Lord.

"Ummm... That's so nice of you to say." *It totally isn't so nice of him to say! What is he thinking? Who calls a total stranger beautiful and then tells her she is sexy? Does this usually work for him?*

He isn't unattractive or anything, but he has no skills! He might as well club me over the head and drag me off to his cave while grunting, "Woman...Mine."

"Maybe, when we get back to the states..." he starts, but I've had enough.

99

"Look, I'm sure you are a nice guy but my husband wouldn't like the direction this conversation is going." I lift my chin, purse my lips, and narrow my eyes at him. I'm hoping this makes me come across as a snooty bitch.

"Husband? Now, little girl, I don't see a wedding ring on that finger. I think you're just joshing with me. Are you trying to make this game a little more interesting?"

Hell no.

"Actually, I don't wear my ring when I travel because it's fucking huge and my very protective, very large husband worries it's an invitation to the less than honest people in this world. But I did notice you slipping your wedding ring off and sliding it into your pocket a few minutes ago. How does Mrs. Greg feel about you trying to hook up with girls half your age when she isn't around to keep you in line?"

"You don't know anything about me, Missy!"

"And I'd like to keep it that way."

He's turning an alarming shade of red. *Should I be worried? Should I call the stewardess? Please don't let him have a heart attack or need some type of resuscitation. My patience is at its end.*

His breathing becomes more regular eventually and he turns away from me, as much as his bulk will allow, when another female sits on his opposite side. I'm tempted to warn her but instead, decide to shift toward the window and lean my head back against the headrest. I'd already tried doing a good deed and that had backfired miserably. She's on her own.

The prescription is really kicking in now and I feel my eyelids getting heavier. Their weight is almost unbearable and my last conscious sensation is that of weightlessness as the plane lifts into the air.

100

Chapter Fourteen: Liv
I Had To See You

"Liv!"

I hear her screeching before I can even see her. Of course, finding her isn't easy when she's a head shorter than almost everyone else in the crowded airport. Before I realize what's happening, Charli collides into me with the force of a hurricane. Together, with her arms tethering us into a single entity of unstoppable motion, we take out a young businessman and two teenagers before slamming into the brick wall that divides the terminal from passenger pick up.

"Ow!"

"Oh, stop complaining! This is your fault for leaving and being gone so long!" she sobs into my hair.

I don't usually give a damn what anyone thinks of me but we're causing a huge scene and I've never been so happy to see Logan in my life. He's finally caught up with his crazy wife and manages to pull her off, at least long enough for me to grab a much-needed intake of oxygen.

"Hey, Liv," he says as he bends down and places a quick kiss on the top of my head. "Forgive Charli. It's all the hormones she has to take."

"I didn't do anything that needs to be forgiven!" Charli insists as she lightly slaps his arm and scowls. Logan gives her that big goofy grin she loves in response.

"And I did?" I ask her.

"Yes!" she sniffs, wiping the tears off her cheeks with the back of her hand. "But the important thing is you're finally home and you are NEVER leaving like that again. Got it?"

"Got it," I promise.

We head over to baggage claim and as we wait for my luggage, I steal covert glances at my best friend.

She looks awful! This baby mess has taken its toll. Always small, she is now painfully thin and there are dark smudges under her eyes. I shoot a glare at Logan over her head when she isn't looking and he seems to understand my concerns. It's then that I notice how affected he is. They both look so stressed and anxious that any minor problem will push them off the cliff.

I should have come home sooner. I knew Charli wasn't coping well and I haven't been here for her. What kind of friend am I?

"Liv?" her voice is soft and she looks me straight in the eyes. "Don't you dare take on any blame for my situation. I'm fine. I'm just a little emotional and happy to see you. I've missed you so much... but I'm glad you went."

"You are?" I ask skeptically. *Hadn't she contradicted this earlier when she'd insisted I was the one needing her forgiveness?*

"Yes. It was an amazing opportunity and I know you needed..." her voice trails off while she tries to think of how to continue, "I know you needed to get away for a little while. But you're home now and I think you'll be surprised by some things."

"Really? Like what?"

She flashes a quick, knowing smile and stays completely silent.

"Logan?" I turn to him for an answer.

"Don't look at me!" he insists but I can tell he knows something.

On our ride back to the apartment above the bar that we will once again share, I'm quiet as I look out the car's window. The landscape is both familiar and foreign. Life had gone on without me, after all. My city had changed in small ways and I guess I had too.

Even though I joked about everyone being available to greet me when I arrived home, I'd been kidding. I'm surprised and touched when I open the rear entrance doors to The Crash and see all of my family and friends. *This must be the surprise Charli and Logan had hinted at earlier.*

Choking back the threat of embarrassing tears isn't easy but I'm determined. I won't have them thinking I've turned into a blubbering baby during my lengthy absence.

"Hello, gorgeous," Kyle whispers as he squeezes me in a fierce hug that lasts long enough for Charli to start rolling her eyes. "You can't imagine how boring a shift can get when you aren't here to bitch about everything," he adds.

"Well yes, I'm sure everything sucked without me around," I agree.

"About damn time," Ronan barks. He comes up right in front of me, with arms folded over his chest, and scowls with all the affection and tenderness I expect from him. "I know you have a few things left to do for this work assignment but you need to get your ass back to work soon. The new girl is..."

"Madison is doing a great job, Ronan! Let her alone," Charli chides.

"Livvy-Loo!" Mom rushes over and when I smell the sweet vanilla of her shampoo and feel the softness of her cheek against mine, it's the closest I've come to truly bawling. Then, Momma D joins us and adds her arms to the group hug that reinforces how much I'm loved.

Eventually, I also receive assurances of how much I've been missed from Kelly and Scott. I even feel generous enough to sit down on the floor and play with their twin daughters, Sophia, and Isabella, before finding my way back to the adults at the bar.

"Liv?" I turn when I hear Charli behind me.

"Yeah?"

"Let's go talk for a minute." She points to a secluded table in the corner, so I follow her.

What's going on? Are she and Logan doing okay? Has she heard something new about her fertility issues? "Alright hooker, you're scaring me. What's up?" I ask, trying to keep the concern out of my voice.

"Can we talk about Zac?"

"Hell no!" I feel the heat of anger surge through me. I thought she wanted to confide something, not badger me about a past I've managed to forget. *Well, maybe forget isn't exactly accurate but I'm working on it. I'll get there if she doesn't decide to bring him up all the time.*

Charli places her hand on my arm to prevent me from leaving the table and waits for me to calm down. "I found it," she says.

"What the hell are you talking about?" *She isn't making any sense.*

"His picture... When Logan and I carried your bags upstairs,

104

this…" She reaches into her pocket and pulls out the photograph. It's a 4x5 print with curled and frayed edges that look well worn. It shows an incredibly attractive man, laughing, wearing a tuxedo, holding a champagne glass and looking right at the camera.

"You had no right to go through my things!" I snatch the photograph out of her hand and slide it into my back pocket. I'm aggravated but mostly embarrassed.

"I didn't!" Her face is furious at my accusation. "It fell out of the front of your backpack. You know I would never snoop. How dare you…" And then her anger turns to tears. "Liv, I'm sorry. I really thought you were over him but then the picture fell out and I…"

I don't think I'm going to be able to deal with this new Charli. My strong, independent friend has become a total whiny girly-girl. *How bad is it going to get when she finally is knocked up?*

"Oh, stop the waterworks, Charli. I beg you. I'm not mad. Just forget about it, okay?"

"But, Liv… you need to know something important about Zac. He is…"

"Stop!" I interrupt, loudly. "I never want to talk about Zachary Reynolds again!"

"Well, would you be willing to talk *to* me, if not about me?"

My intake of breath is lightning fast and loud. The exhalation that should follow doesn't come. Blood rushes to my cheeks and causes a pounding in my skull and my whole body begins to tremble. I'd heard his voice in my imagination, and in my dreams, for more than a year and a half but now he's standing right behind me.

Why?

Turning slowly and trying to regain my composure, I raise my chin until I can see his face. *Oh, that face…* My imagination had never done it justice.

"Hello, Liv," he says softly and the deep timbre of his voice sends me right back to the night we kissed, the night he'd held me... the night I'd been trying to run from.

Charli jumps up. "Ummm..." Even though I beg her with my eyes to stay and rescue me, she flees the table like her ass is on fire. "I'll let you two...ummm...yeah..." she calls over her shoulder before disappearing completely.

"Zac, I don't think this is a good idea." I start to leave but he places one hand on my shoulder and gently presses until I lower back to my seat.

"Please, Liv." He walks around and sits in the chair vacated by Charli.

She and I will be having a long talk about friendship and loyalty very soon.

"What are you doing here?" I can't imagine why he would come. *And where is his wife?*

"I had to see you," he tells me like that's a reasonable excuse for his presence. *Doesn't he get that he shouldn't be here?*

"Oh, okay... well, that clears everything up! Of course, you *had* to see the woman that made friends with your wife, photographed your *wedding* and then proceeded to suck your face right after your fucking honeymoon. That's totally logical. Now that you've seen me, it's time you leave."

"Stop it. Just listen to me, damn it!"

"Fine!" I cross my arms under my chest, narrow my eyes and pinch my mouth into a tight line of anger. Instead of being impressed by my fierce expression, he laughs at me.

"God, how I missed you." He brings one hand up and rubs the back of his neck. I just stare with my mouth hanging open.

"Don't say that to me. You can't say that to me. I've done just

106

fine getting over you and you don't get to walk into *my* party and say that kind of shit and make me miss you all over again. It isn't fair."

"Liv..."

"No! Listen to me! You are *married*. You made a vow before God, your friends, and your family to love, honor and cherish Sabrina. I can't do this. How can you expect me to?"

"It's not like that!"

"Yes, yes it is like that!" I slam back my chair and stand up.

"Liv!" Zac stands too and tries to maneuver around the table to get to me but I know if he touches me, my resolve will crumble. I bolt from the room and run for the metal stairs that lead to my apartment on the second floor.

Just before I slide the lock in place, I hear him yelling my name again. Then I hear Ronan telling everyone the party is over and to go home.

Chapter Fifteen: Liv
Does That Mean I Can Kiss You?

I look at the picture of Zac for the last time, knowing this goodbye is long overdue. My obsession has to end. Instead of getting on with my life and learning to live without something that was never mine anyway, I held on. I really believed my time away would rid me of my want for him. Seeing him again had proved how foolish that belief was. If I'd only been physically attracted to him, it might have done the trick. But no, I'm not that lucky. The more time I spent in his company, discovering the man behind the beautiful body and perfect face, the more I wanted him.

How twisted is it that the time we were together was because I was photographing the start of his life with someone else?

I close my eyes and force my hands to make the first small tear in the worn photograph. It rips more than just the gloss-coated paper, it rips a little corner of my heart. By the time the photograph is a pile of confetti on my comforter, I feel hollow and unmoored.

We never had the chance to get to know one another like I'd wanted.

We weren't able to date or see if the attraction could be the start of something more meaningful. By the time we met, Zac belonged to someone else. By the time we kissed, he had already made a commitment to love another woman. I don't even have the comfort of being able to hate the woman he chose because she's kind and funny and had become my friend. Zac and I have no future. Our future ended before it started.

I lie on top of the scraps of the photo and pull my pillow tightly over my face. I scream. I scream out of frustration and anger. I scream out of misery and sadness.

Once my throat is raw and my screams have been exchanged for deep, even breaths, I sense something isn't right. Without looking, I know someone is in the room with me. Assuming Charli has let herself in -*she does live here too*- I take a big gulp of air, slide the pillow to the side and sit up.

But it's not Charli in my room. It's Zac.

"How the hell did you get in here?" *I know I locked the door. He shouldn't be here.*

"Charli gave me the key. She and Logan are staying at Scott and Kelly's tonight so we can talk."

I really thought Charli was my best friend and loved me enough to help me do the right thing. And I know Zac and Logan have been friends since childhood but how could they conspire together to hurt Sabrina like this?

"You need to leave, Zac."

"Not until you hear me out," he begs, "Please just listen to me."

"I got your email. It's okay. I know you feel bad for that night but I didn't run off because of you," I lie. "It was a career choice. So you are hereby absolved of all guilt. Feel better?"

"No. I'm not looking for forgiveness. I want your understanding."

"Whatever. Fine. I understand. It was a moment of weakness and we had too much to drink. Ordinarily, you would never have kissed me."

"I've wanted to kiss you since the first time I saw you... almost two and half years ago," he confides.

I start to tremble. "I haven't known you that long."

"No, but that was the first time I *saw* you. You were standing across the room, in a dark green dress, and you were so exquisite I almost convinced myself I was dreaming. And then you laughed..." He closes his eyes for a brief moment and smiles at the memory. "Sabrina returning to my side was all that saved me from plowing across that room and trying to convince you to leave with me."

Saying her name breaks the spell woven by his words. "Go home to your wife. I won't do this, Zac."

"I don't have a wife, Liv."

His words make no sense. My heart wants to race with joy but my brain knows better than to buy into the illusion of what I want to hear. "I'm pretty sure you paid me a hell of a lot of money to photograph your wedding. Sabrina loves you, and you love her. Go home."

"Sabrina and I got divorced. It was final three months ago."

Okay, that's it. Someone drugged me on the plane. *Maybe it was the perv sitting next to me?* I'm probably still on the plane, just having some sort of psychotic breakdown.

"If that's true..." I trail off, unsure of how to process this information.

"It is true. Do you really think Charli and Logan would let me in here if I were still married? Hell, Logan would kick my ass for being a cheater. Charli would finish me off for trying to seduce you while being married!"

"So... you're trying to seduce me?" His answering smirk is cute. I feel the urge to tackle him down onto the bed with me and seduce *him*.

"I'm trying to tell you that I'm single and if you are willing to give me a chance, I would love to get to know you. I might be a little obsessed with you too... but if that freaks you out, forget that part."

"Oh," I whisper, and for the second time in my life, I'm at a loss for words. *How does he do this to me?*

"Can we give this a try?" he asks.

"Maybe..."

"Maybe?" He sighs in frustration and comes to sit next me on the bed.

"What happened with Sabrina?" I ask. "I'm not trying to pry or open any wounds but this is very recent and when you consider our history... I need to know. Was it my fault? Did you tell her about the kiss?" I'm scared of his answer but I have to know.

"No." He takes both of my hands into his and holds them together on his lap. "I've loved Sabrina since high school. I still do. I always will."

His words sting and I struggle to pull my hands back. He tightens his grip.

"But loving her wasn't enough," he continues. "I wasn't 'in love' with her anymore. As soon as we made a serious commitment, we realized we wanted different things from life. She is beautiful and wonderful. I want everything good for her but not with me. She feels the same."

His words start the tiniest of flutters in my heart but I wait to hear it all. I have to know everything.

"I thought that after we got married, we would start a family. We've been together a long time. Why should we wait? A s you know, when we returned from our honeymoon she told me she doesn't want kids at all. I hoped she would change her mind. The more time passed, the more firmly she knew it wasn't what she wanted. For me, it was a deal breaker."

"You didn't decide something that important *before* the wedding?" I find it difficult to swallow that anyone would pledge their life to someone without first making sure they want the same things.

"We did," he asserts. "Of course, we did. She says she really thought that, in time, she'd want kids. She felt the desire to be a mother was a natural need and that the maternal instinct would kick in eventually. I hoped it would. After Mikey had stayed with us for a couple of weeks, she changed her opinion."

"Mikey?" I'm trying to keep my temper in check but for fuck's sake, how could a precious boy like Mikey cause her to decide she didn't want kids? If anything, he should have shown her how wonderful being a mother could be!

"Don't be angry with her, she just…"

"How can I not be angry? Mikey is an awesome kid!"

"No arguments from me. I love him, Liv. Sabrina does too. My parents took a much-needed vacation, so Mikey stayed with us. There weren't any problems. We all had a great time together."

"Then why did she decide kids suck?"

His chuckle is light and his eyes are soft when he reaches out to tuck an errant strand of hair behind my ear. "She doesn't think kids suck. She knows how important it is to make your children your priority and the incredible responsibility it is to raise them into happy, healthy adults. She's not a selfish person. If we had a baby, I know she would devote herself to being a good mother but she wouldn't feel fulfilled or satisfied by that life. She loves her career and doesn't want to give it up. It's wrong to expect her to push it to the background. That's not fair to her or a child."

"That sounds like a lot of outdated and ridiculous bullshit to me. Women can be mothers and have careers! You have your restaurant but I know you'd be an incredible father."

"Thanks. I will always love what I do but my baby would come first. Always. Sabrina just doesn't think she'd feel the same. She told me that even if I closed the restaurant and was the primary caregiver, she still doesn't want to be a parent. Also, there is always the knowledge that when my parents pass away, I'll get Mikey. I'm glad to do it. I suppose to most women, I come with baggage."

"He isn't baggage! He's a bonus, in my book. I agree that no one should have a kid because it's expected. It's good she figured it out now but I'm sorry it came between you." He might not believe me but it's true. I would never hope for someone's marriage to fail.

"Thank you. I sure never factored myself into the divorce statistic. It sucks but it really is best for both of us."

"Where is Sabrina now?"

"She took the manager position at her company's new workout facility and spa. They just opened in Los Angeles. She loves it."

"She's not even in our city?"

"No."

"You are absolutely certain you aren't married?" I sound like an idiot. Even with his explanation, I'm having difficulty believing it.

"I'm not married, Liv."

"Does that mean I can kiss you?" I whisper softly.

It's all the invitation he needs. Before I can blink, he leans forward. Releasing my hands from his lap, he buries his long fingers into my hair and pulls me closer. I feel the hot pressure of his lips against mine.

It's not enough. I need more.

My hands roam over his strong, broad shoulders and down his back. I swear I feel his groan when I open my mouth and run my tongue along his lips to gain entrance. Knowing that I can finally kiss him without guilt is so unbelievably satisfying.

I grab the hem of his T-shirt to yank it up but he captures my hands to stop them.

"Liv, we don't have to..."

"Shut the fuck up, Zac."

Laughing, he closes his eyes and lets me have my way with him. I successfully remove and toss his shirt to give me the access I crave. I run the tips of my fingers down the rigid contours of his chest and abdomen. Letting myself dip low enough to skim the edge of his waistband, I hear his deep intake of breath and smile. When he finally opens his eyes again, it's just in time to see me unzip the back of my dress and let it drop.

Taking his hands, I guide them behind me to unclasp my bra. When it falls between us, his chocolate eyes darken to near black and molten lava courses through my veins.

"They're real," he says in awe.

"Damn straight," I assure him, and he grins like he just won first prize.

Our breathing is becoming loud and frantic. My heart beats

double time as we shed the rest of our clothing and I manage to get my first real look at his naked perfection. It's all I'd imagined and more, a lot more.

"Liv?" His husky voice barely registers. I'm a busy girl right now.

"What?" I answer in reflex. My attention is fixated on the pleasure I'm deriving from the small nibbles and tongue strokes I'm using to explore every inch of him.

"We have all night," he promises. "We can take our time."

I pause and his frown contradicts his words. "Let me explain something to you, Zac." I want no confusion over what I need right now. "I've been dying to do this since the beginning. I truly believed it would never happen. I don't know what will come to-morrow, next week or next year but right now you are in my bed and naked. I'm going to have you before anything tries to take you away and ruin my dreams again. Got it?"

"I like the sound of that."

"Then you're going to love this." I push him onto his back and position myself above him. When I lean in to run my tongue from the hard edge of his jaw to the shallow indention of his navel, his whole body convulses. I feel the deep joy of knowing he wants me as much as I want him.

"Oh, shit!" I sit up abruptly and he groans when the heat between my thighs falls to rest fully upon him.

"For the love of... Why did you stop?" he implores and it sounds like he is in agony as he continues to move beneath me. He's trying to position me for invasion.

"Where's your wallet?"

"My wallet?" He is so confused. "Are you robbing me? Because you can have whatever the hell you want, just don't stop!" He reaches for my hips with insistence and I playfully bat his hands away.

"No, jackass. We need a condom."

That stops all activity. His eyes widen with understanding. "Shit," he mutters and runs a hand down his face.

"You don't have one?" I almost screech. My chest is hot and tight and I can't seem to get enough air.

"No! I didn't come here tonight to jump you!"

"Well, why not? Damn it!" I scream back and he laughs. I don't see anything remotely funny about our situation.

"Don't you have one?" he asks.

"I've been gone for over a year! I haven't had sex in forever. Contrary to what it looks like right now, I'm not a skank!"

"I know that! Shit... What about Charli and Logan? Would there be one in their room?"

My face must have asked "are you stupid" pretty plainly because his desperate groan of awareness is quick. "No," he answers himself. "Of course not. They're trying to get pregnant and have no use for birth control."

"Zac, we could just..."

"What? Please don't say we have to wait!"

There are always other things we can do but damn I want all of him. Once again, something is trying to prevent it. I make a decision. "I'm on the pill," I admit.

"Are you sure?"

"Yes, I'm *sure* I'm on the pill," I deadpan.

He groans like I'm not funny.   *We both know I am.* "Are you sure you want to do this?" he corrects.

I respond by lowering myself onto him and watching his eyes roll back into his head.

"Okay," he mumbles.

"Okay," I agree.

We slowly find our rhythm and learn how of our bodies work together. He grabs my hand and places sweet kisses on the inside of my wrist but right now I've lost all patience with sweet. I grab his shoulders and encourage him to sit up, with me still wrapped around him.

Raking my nails down his back gets the reaction I want and our pace becomes furious and all consuming. Within minutes, my vision goes dark around the edges and my body has disconnected from my conscious self. It does what it's been made for. When my head falls back and I scream out his name, I forgive Charli and Logan for all the nights I've lost sleep because of them.

We collapse together in a boneless heap, still unwilling to disconnect from one another. I know he was worth the frustration, the pain, and the heartache. I've fallen for him and he was so worth the wait.

Chapter Sixteen: Zac

Let's Try This Date Thing You Speak Of

Sunlight spills across her porcelain skin and turns her hair to flames. I've been awake for almost an hour but I'm perfectly content just to watch her. The night had given me something I'd never realized I was missing. With her tightly tucked against my side and secured by my arm, one slender leg hitched up over my thigh, I match my breathing to hers and relive last night. Nothing in my life has ever made me feel this kind of hope.

I love the way she mumbles softly in her sleep. She will probably kill me if I mention it but even her soft, snuffling snores are cute. Several minutes ago, she had stirred and thrashed about, pulling at the covers and causing me to tense. It hadn't lasted long but made me wonder about her dreams.

Yesterday I was determined to talk to her. I wanted to explain how my situation had changed and apologize again for my behavior that night at my restaurant. I will never forgive myself for making her run. I wasn't lying when I told her that my intention wasn't seduction. I didn't dare to dream I would have that chance. Today, anything is possible.

I've resisted for as long as I can. Gently, barely touching her at all, I use the tip of my index finger to trace the outline of her generous lips. A slow grin settles on her face, and even though her eyes are closed, I smile at her.

Then, quick as whip, those delicious lips part. She sucks my finger into her mouth and bites.

"Ow!"

"Serves you right for disturbing my sleep," she grumbles without opening her eyes.

"It's not my fault. You shouldn't be lying here, looking so damn irresistible. I'm only a man."

"Hmmmm," she frowns, "Are you accusing me of being a temptress?"

Rolling her body to face away, I pull her backside tight against me. I let her feel just how tempting she is. Instead of conversation, we find other ways to communicate.

While our first time had been the culmination of the heat and passion we'd had to deny, our morning encounter is slow, lazy and a lesson in the joys of taking your time.

"I could get used to this," I tell her.

"Sex? Yeah, it's not a bad way to start your day. I mean, it's not chocolate but it has its merit."

"I didn't mean the sex!" I playfully nip at her shoulder.

"Oh... So, no more sex?" she asks with a sultry smirk.

I groan and she laughs. "I meant, I like waking up with you trying to burrow into my side."

"I get cold when I sleep. Any warm body would have done the job."

"Uh huh."

"Zac?" she whispers and her suddenly serious tone makes me nervous.

"Yes?"

"I need something," she confesses.

"Anything, Liv. What can I do?"

"I need you to get your heavy-ass arm off of me so I can get up and pee."

Laughing, I help her extricate herself from our tangle of limbs. As she walks out of the room, I can't take my eyes off of her. She is flawless. Full, heavy breasts - that I still can't believe are real - a tiny waist and gently curved hips balance her frame perfectly. Obviously, I know what a naked woman looks like but this naked woman has brought me to my knees.

Actually, being on my knees could present a few interesting options I'd like to try out soon.

My life had been all planned out since graduation. I had been a good student, had loved culinary school and had worked hard to open my own restaurant. When Sabrina and I had met, we had instantly clicked. Our relationship was founded on respect and love for one another. The next step had been marriage and children. After meeting Liv, I became aware of the cracks in our foundation. It wasn't Liv's fault. They already existed but she brought them to the surface. My life now has the potential to go from safe and peaceful to a wild, passionate adventure. I'm excited to see what each new day will bring.

Liv's been gone for longer than expected when the smell of coffee floats into the room and clues me in to the cause of her delay. Following the scent, I grab my boxer briefs, pull them on and head into the main living space.

Now wrapped in a black silk, kimono robe with a pink cherry

blossom design, she's leaning against the small counter in her kitchen pouring a large mug of coffee.

"I hate coffee but I know you like it, so I stole some of Charli's for you," she tells me.

"Thanks." I walk closer, take the mug away and set it near the sink. Picking her up by her tiny waist, I set her on the counter in front of me. Separating her knees, I wedge my body between them and wrap my arms around her. I kiss her. It starts out slow but builds to a passionate obliteration of my senses. Slowly, we pull back and smile at one another as I run my fingers through her hair languidly. I love the feel of the red satin curls as they straighten and spring back with each gentle tug.

"Where do we go from here?" she finally asks.

"Well..." I consider her question. "Maybe, since we had sex... it was fucking amazing by the way and I am looking forward to doing it again... should we go on a date?"

She purses her lips into an adorable pucker and looks toward the ceiling in contemplation of the idea I've presented. "A date?"

"Yeah, you know, dinner and a movie? Tickets to a show or an afternoon at the museum? A date, Liv."

She looks right at me and grins. "Okay. Let's try this date thing you speak of."

I smile in answer. "Tonight I have to work late at the restaurant but maybe tomorrow we could..."

"Shit!" Her interruption startles me.

"Is something wrong?" *Is she mad I have to work tonight? Has she changed her mind about us going out?*

"I can't go out tomorrow night," she explains.

"Oh, that's okay. We can find another..."

"No, Zac. I'm leaving in the morning for..."

"You're leaving!" I know I sound pissed. "You just got home!

121

I thought we were good. Why would you leave again?" My heart tightens in my chest and I'm finding it hard to act calm and rational. She doesn't owe me anything. We aren't even in a relationship yet. If I act possessive and freak her out, we may never make it that far.

"Calm down! It's just for a few weeks!"

She's laughing at me. *I don't think this is funny at all.*

"Why are you leaving again?"

"I have one last assignment to complete this job. I will be in Seattle, at the main office of the organization that hired me. I have to complete all the edits and help with the design layout of my images. It shouldn't take more than two or three weeks at most and then I'm home for good."

"Three weeks?" Why do those three weeks sound like three years?

"At most! I promise." She quiets my arguments by kissing me again. "We're finally together. I don't want to go. I'll miss you. This time, we'll talk and sext and..."

"Sext?" I whisper into her ear.

"Definitely, until we are together again and we can take that "t" off."

Chapter Seventeen: Liv

Damn the "Feels"

"Hey, you," I say in my sexiest voice.

"Hello, beautiful."

His words cause a minor commotion in my chest. It's just an endearment and a pretty generic one at that. Just by the virtue of being able to hear it without the guilt, it does all sorts of warm, tender things to me. I've never felt things like this before, had feared I never would, and now all those sappy love songs and ridiculous Nicholas Sparks movies make sense to me. *Damn Zac and the 'feels.'*

"How was your day?" I ask. *That's a normal thing to ask the guy you think you're falling for, had mind blowing sex with a couple of times and still haven't gone out on a date with, isn't it?*

"I was very thankful for my efficient staff today," he responds.

"Oh?"

"Yes. They managed to keep my restaurant running smoothly and my customers happy while I walked around dazed and smiling at nothing in particular. I'm suffering from a serious lack of focus."

"I'm not sure I can accept a date with someone that can't focus. After all, I deserve a man that can give all his attention to me."

"Then you're in luck because being focused on you is the only thing I am capable of apparently. It was the root of all my trouble today."

I giggle. *For the love of all that is holy, I giggled.* I don't giggle. I laugh, smirk or more often... scoff. He's turned me into a pre-teen crushing on a boy band.

"How long until you come home?" His voice drops and all thoughts of giggles disappear. I remember the look on his face when I touched him and the feel of his warm skin all over me. I swallow hard.

"I've only been gone a week, Zac," I remind him in soft tones to match his.

"It's been eight days actually but it feels like a lot longer."

"I know. I should be able to come home the week after next." I love what I do and I'd loved this assignment but right now all I want to do it grab the next flight out of this rainy place.

He groans into his phone and I laugh with sympathy.

"Mikey says you need to come home now," he says.

"Low blow! Don't bring Mikey into this."

"I will use any means necessary to get what I want," he assures me. "Besides, he really does want to see you. You're all he talks about and if I didn't feel the same way, I'd get jealous that he prefers you to me now."

I think of the young man that holds a special chunk of my heart. I hate that I didn't have time to visit him before heading to Seattle but it's the first thing I plan on doing when I get back home. *Well, maybe the second.* "I love all the pictures he sent me while I was gone."

"You have no idea how hard it was every time I went to see him. My marriage was in crisis but you were still in my thoughts all the time. Even though I knew the right thing was to forget about you, I couldn't. I'd go to spend time with my little brother and all he wanted to talk about was his red-haired Liv, his pretty and funny Liv and his perfect Liv. All I wanted was for you to be *my* Liv."

His Liv? I like the sound of that and it scares me to death. I'd had several boyfriends throughout the years but no one that I'd felt I belonged to, no one I'd wanted to belong to. "Zac..."

"Yes."

"I..." *Shit. What do I say?* I don't love him, it's too soon for that. I feel something but I don't know how to tell him.

"Liv?"

"I..." *Damn it, Liv! Find your tongue!* "I have to get ready for work."

It's a total cop-out. I mean, I do have to get ready for work but I'm just not ready to explain to him how I feel yet. I can't even explain it to myself.

"Okay, I better do the same," he says and then adds, "Send me a picture."

"What?" *What kind of picture does he want? Does he mean the Seattle skyline or an image from my assignment?*

"A picture of you, right now. I want to see you. I need to see you."

He wants me to take a selfie? "I look like shit. I haven't even put my makeup on yet!"

"I don't care. I keep picturing how you looked that morning, lying in bed with no makeup, and even better no clothes. That image is what keeps me hiding out in my office or carrying a large wait tray in front me all day."

The idea of Zac walking around greeting his customers and employees, while hiding his lower half with a big round tray, brings on a new wave of laughter. "Okay. I'll send a picture but you can't share it with anyone. I swear if it ends up on a social media site, you'll never have the opportunity to create some new visuals with me. Is that clear?"

"Crystal!"

"Okay... Hang on a minute."

I switch my phone's camera to face me and scowl at the screen. I wish I had time to put at least a little mascara on... but then a plan emerges. Holding the phone a little higher and angling it down, I loosen the belt of my robe until I have a good six inches of cleavage showing. If it were any lower, there'd be no need for his imagination. I snap a couple of pictures and choose my favorite. It shows some of my face in the top right corner, but the star of the show is definitely the girls. I figure that will distract him enough to give my clean-scrubbed face a quick pass over. Hopefully, it will also prevent him from wanting to share the picture with anyone. He's made it clear he's territorial about what he considers his.

I attach it to an outgoing text message, double checking that it's addressed to his name and number, and hit send.

Within seconds, my phone actually vibrates in my hand from the intensity of his groans. "You're killing me!" he says deeply. His voice does funny things to my southern hemisphere.

"Bye, Zac," I say in a breathy voice of exaggerated huskiness, putting on my best Marilyn Monroe impersonation.

"Liv!"

126

I'm laughing as I hang up, but he isn't content to let it go that easily. My phone starts blowing up with texts of all the things he's planning to do to me when I finally come home.

Chapter Eighteen: Liv
Absolutely Not Possible

"I'm losing my shit out here, Charli!" I tell her for the third time.

"Calm down, you get to come home tomorrow," she reminds me for the fourth time.

"I know but it's been so frustrating." I'm not usually a complainer but my "two to three-week wrap-up job" has ended up being four weeks and two days. Phone calls, texts messages and a slew of increasingly naughty pictures between Zac and I have been fun but not as much fun as we could be having in person.

"I think part of it is this awful weather. I haven't felt like myself since getting here," I whine. *Sure Liv, blame the weather. Unsatisfied lust is my real issue.*

"I know you said it has been chilly and rainy almost every day. Are you congested? You sound okay."

"No, I'm breathing fine. Maybe it's just all the room service?

I'm so tired after work that I just come back to my room, order something random and then crash out. Maybe they gave me food poisoning or something?"

"Have you had your morning cereal? Maybe that will improve your mood. I can't even talk to you before breakfast usually," she suggests. I appreciate that she's trying to help.

"No, actually I feel kind of nauseous and don't want anything right now."

"Oh," she says softly. It puts me on alert.

"What's wrong, Charli?" Her voice is getting thick and I'm pretty sure I already know.

"I was just thinking how nice it would be to have a reason to feel nauseous in the morning. Instead, I had to send Logan out for tampons."

"Oh God, I'm so sorry. I wish there were something I could do!" I hate feeling helpless. She and Logan deserve to be parents and it's so unfair that it isn't happening for them.

"You would think I'd be used to this by now. Somehow you never get used to it."

"Don't give up! You can do this. I just know it." Getting tough with her sometimes helps to bring her mood up a little but it doesn't seem to be helping much this morning.

"It's the most awful feeling, knowing that women get pregnant every day accidentally and I can't, no matter how hard I try."

"Have you guys talked about adoption or a surrogate?" I've never brought this up before but I can hear her desperation.

"Some. If we have to go that route, then we will. We *will* be parents someday, no matter what it takes but I want to carry my child. I want to feel my baby move inside me. I want to experience childbirth."

"Well, now I know you're off your rocker. If I ever decide to make a baby, they can just knock me out and take that kid while I'm unconscious!"

This finally brings a laugh and I feel relieved. "Thanks, Liv. I love you."

"Ugh! Don't get all mushy on me, hooker! I'll see you tomorrow."

"Okay, bye."

"Bye."

I hang up the phone and fall backward across my bed. *How would I feel in her position?* I'm a long way off from wanting to start a family but when the time comes, I will want to be able to carry my child inside me too.

I roll to my side and yawn while trying to get motivated enough to start my day. Even though I'd crashed before ten o'clock last night, I'm still exhausted and it sucks. Determined to get my ass in gear, I stand up but a wave of nausea hits so hard I sink back down on the edge of the bed. *What the hell?* I'd been kidding about the food poisoning but maybe it's a real possibility.

Then Charli's words come back to me. She wished she had a reason to be nauseated in the mornings.

No. It's absolutely not possible. I shouldn't even be thinking such a thing. It's impossible.

I'm on the pill for fuck's sake! You don't get... Shit, I can't even think the word. You don't get "in that condition" when you are on birth control and only have sex a couple of times!

But I know, actually, you can.

After my stomach calms down enough to get up, I go to the bathroom. I drink a glass of water and place a cool rag on the back of my neck. Throwing on a pair of sweatpants, my furry boots, and a hoodie, I head out to the drugstore across the street from the hotel.

Half an hour later, I'm sitting crossed legged on my bathroom floor, surrounded by twenty-two little sticks with two pink lines showing in the plastic window. I start to cry.

Chapter Nineteen: Zac

My Bruised Soul

The glass shatters as it hits the brick wall of my office. When my assistant manager opens the door out of concern, I'm a total dick and yell at her to get the fuck out. I've probably lost the respect of my entire staff today but I can't even take the time to worry about it. I'll figure something out later.

I handled the disintegration of my marriage better than I'd handled today's phone call from Liv. I'm furious. I'm so pissed at her at this moment that it's probably a good thing she's still in Seattle.

At the same time, I'm so broken hearted I want to shut out the entire world. *How could she do this? Why did she do this?*

The last four weeks have been sweet torture and all I've done is count the seconds until she's back here with me. I daydream of holding her. The memories of her velvet skin and the wild sounds she makes when I'm buried inside her, haunt my nights.

Tomorrow was supposed to be perfect. Her flight will land at four o'clock in the afternoon and I had planned on being there. I wanted to take her home, cook for her and then spend all night learning exactly every inch of this crazy woman I've fallen for.

Instead, she'd called me today and said she was very sorry. She's decided it would be best if we don't see each other for a while.

What am I supposed to do with that?

Last night, she told me in great detail all the things she plans to do to my body and sends me a picture. It was the most erotically beautiful thing I've ever seen. Forever a photographer, even her selfies are pieces of art.

Now she doesn't want to see me. She won't even take my calls. *What in the hell had happened? Had she met someone else in Seattle?*

That seems unlikely when you consider how abruptly she's cut me out of her life. My only logical conclusion is that she thought about our situation last night and has changed her mind. It's almost time for her to come home and while we've had some fun, she doesn't want a real relationship with me.

It's a conclusion that hurts deep enough to bruise my soul.

Chapter Twenty: Liv

It Was an Accident

I left the rain of Seattle to come to a torrential downpour that cuts almost parallel to the earth. It soaks even the people prepared enough to have umbrellas. It's dark and gloomy, a perfect fit for my mood.

Rolling my suitcase behind me, oblivious to the raindrops forcefully pelting my skin and saturating my hair, I hail a cab. I ignore his look of disgust as I slide my sodden, miserable self into his backseat. The ride to my apartment is thankfully quiet, I'm not in the mood for a chatty cabbie, and I tip him generously to make up for the puddles I leave behind on his upholstery.

I knock before sliding my key into the door and entering. I want to give Charli and Logan a little warning. They expect me to be at Zac's tonight and even with the knock, my entrance causes Charli to startle.

"Liv?" Her voice is soft and alarmed.

I must look like I have the plague. "Hey." It's not much of a greeting, but it's all I can manage.

"Why are you here? What happened?" She sets her laptop on the trunk we use for a coffee table and walks over to me. I sink to the floor and cry. I've never cried as much as I have since knowing Zac. I hate it.

Ignoring the water that will migrate into her thin T-shirt and sweats, she goes down to her knees and wraps both arms around me. I lay my head on her bony shoulder and let my fear for my future, grief over what this will do to my relationship with Zac and pure terror over how Charli will handle this news consume me. She's not pushing for answers. She holds me and lets me try to pull myself back together. She has no idea how I'm about to hurt her.

After convincing me to take a hot shower, dressing me in my thick terry robe, and forcing a mug of hot tea into my hands, she guides me to our couch. She then joins me and waits patiently for me to be able to talk.

"Where's Logan?" I croak.

"He's watching the game with Scott. I don't expect him back for some time."

I know it's hard for her to let me take my time. She probably wants to interrogate me and I don't blame her but I don't know how to begin.

"I asked Zac not to come to the airport," I finally admit.

"Oh," she says in confusion. "Okay."

"I told him that it would best if we spent some time apart."

She absorbs this with surprise but is supportive and waits for me to be ready to share more.

"I just need some time to decide what to do. I don't want him pressuring me into things I'm not ready for," I explain.

"I thought you wanted to give a relationship with him a real try? Didn't you hope it would become more?" she asks tentatively and without judgment.

"I did... but that was before." I feel the pressure of tears building again as I know it's coming closer. *I'm going to share something with my best friend that will tear her open.*

"Before what, Liv?"

"Before..." I take a deep breath and close my eyes. "Before I found out I'm pregnant."

When imagining my revelation to Charli, I'd pictured her tears joining mine. I had expected wracking sobs and shared misery. I have a life altering addition on its way. I'm not ready for it but the cause of my grief would have given her the greatest joy.

I thought I knew my best friend better than anyone else in the world but she surprises me. There are no tears. Instead, she relaxes her muscles until she is no longer holding me and then stands up. Without a backward glance or an uttered sound, she walks to the room she shares with her husband and closes the door behind her.

I'm wholly unprepared for what this does to me.

I hadn't meant to get pregnant.

Deep down I know she understands this but knowing something doesn't make it bearable. For the first time in our lives, she can't stand the sight of me and it completely shatters the little bit of heart I have left.

I always knew that one day I would be a mother but I'd imagined it would happen after years spent in a committed relationship with the man I'd chosen to spend my life with. Zac will be a good father but we can't provide one stable household together. We aren't even together.

I have to tell him.

I know that I have to tell him soon. Our conversations about why his marriage had failed and what he wants out of life had made it perfectly clear how he feels about children. He would probably prefer this happen with his wife or a serious girlfriend but he's one of the good guys. He'll pretend he is thrilled.

It won't surprise me if he tries to convince me we should get married.

I believe in marriage. I believe in lifelong commitment. My moms had shown me how much joy comes from shared lives filled with real love and I won't settle for less. I won't marry any man out of some misbegotten idea of propriety or obligation. If he wants to be a father to his child, he has that right, but for now, I need to focus on me.

The last thing I need is to be pregnant and trying to force a relationship with him because it's expected.

Finding my resolve, I walk to Charli's closed door and knock softly. When there's no response, I try again. After my third attempt, I accept that she's ignoring me and settle for leaning my head against the door's frame.

"Can I come in?" I speak into the tiny crack.

"No," she responds firmly and I flinch.

"Please, Charli. I want you to talk to me." I'm not above begging if necessary. I need my friend and I need to be there for her.

"I just can't right now, Liv," she hisses. I've never heard her sound like this.

"I didn't do it on purpose!" I feel like I'm defending actions I hadn't taken. Circumstances had shaped my future without ever asking my opinion on the matter.

"I know that, but I can't help the way it feels," she admits.

"How does it feel?" I'm speaking softly now but she hears

me.

"Like my best friend betrayed me!" she screams and I jump back, startled.

"It was an accident!" *How can I convince her I didn't mean for this to happen?*

"How lucky for you!" she counters.

"Lucky? You think I'm lucky?" My voice rises to match my agitation. "You're married to a man that loves you and stands by your side no matter what. I'm single and about to have a kid with someone I barely know. Tell me again how lucky I am!"

"At least, you can have a baby! I'm broken and I'll never be able to do more than watch all my friends start popping out kids with an ease they don't even appreciate."

My laugh is bitter. I throw some clean clothes into a small bag and leave. I know she's hurting but so am I. If I stay, I'm afraid we'll say things we can't take back.

Chapter Twenty-One: Liv
The Birds and the Bees

Mom opens the door before I even knock. I called her on my way over, so I guess she's been watching for my car.

"What is it, Liv?" she asks as she pulls me inside and wraps her arms around me. I drop my bag on the floor of the entryway and hug her back.

"Is Momma D home too?" I ask, looking past her into the living room.

"Yes. Come in, baby."

I follow her into the spotlessly clean room and sink down onto the soft, leather couch. I see my other mom is sitting across from me, waiting to see what prompted this unexpected visit. All I'd said on the phone was that we needed to talk.

I'm reminded of when I got into trouble as a teenager and we had to all sit down and discuss my behavior. This feels exactly like that and it pisses me off. *I'm too old to be explaining my mis-*

takes to my parents.

I know the anger is coming from my guilt. They aren't doing anything but waiting patiently for me to share what I'm upset about.

"So..." I begin, but can't think of how to continue.

"Liv, you're scaring us. Just tell us what happened." Momma D is straightforward and I know it's time to just fess up.

"Okay, well...funny story...ummm..." *I'm making a mess of this.*

"Liv," her tone leaves no doubt they've had it with my stalling.

"Fuck it... Guess what?" I say with exaggerated excitement, "You two are going to be grandmothers! How fucking awesome is that?"

These two women have loved and raised me, taught me everything important I need to know and have always known exactly what to say during every bizarre situation I've thrown their way. Today they are completely speechless. They also have identical expressions of shock, which is hilarious on faces that couldn't look more different. Mom is blonde, fair and the perfect model of all natural motherhood. Momma D is deeply dark of hair, skin and eyes. She is so chic she turns heads everywhere she goes. I love my mothers and they love me but their silence is freaking me the hell out.

"Okay..." I stand up, "This went over well. Maybe it's time I just..."

I don't get time to finish my thought as they both jump up and practically attack me. Mom is crying but she's smiling so I take it as a good sign. Momma D is more emotionally reserved like I usually am, but she's still smiling wide enough to split her face.

"A baby!" Mom sighs. "I'm going to be a Grandma."

"I thought you were on the pill?" *Leave it to Momma D to be blunt.*

"I was. I wasn't trying to get knocked up!" I protest.

"Well, I know you are aware of what causes this," she counters.

"Dana!" Mom slaps her shoulder lightly in admonishment.

"What?" she asks innocently. "We told her all about the birds and the bees a long time ago, Carol."

I groan. My sex talk had been unforgettable. Mom, red-faced and embarrassed, was speaking in the most general terms. I had no idea what she was talking about. Momma D had stepped in to explain.

"You need a guy's penis to meet up with your vagina to make babies," she had said without mincing words.

Poor Mom had choked. She'd been trying to take a sip of water when she heard this explanation and we'd had to pound on her back for several minutes. Of course being the daughter of lesbians, this conversation had only created more questions. Trying to explain sperm donors and in vitro fertilization to an eleven-year-old must have been a nightmare. It had taken me several more years to really sort it all out.

"Yeah, I know how I ended up in this situation and yes, I'm on the pill. After talking to my doctor yesterday afternoon, my best guess is the antibiotics I was taking sort of nullified them."

"Well, who is the father?" Mom asks. "I didn't know you were even seeing someone."

"You do know who the father is, right?" Momma D asks, earning herself another shoulder slap from Mom.

I roll my eyes. "Of course, I do!"

"Who is he, honey?" Mom asks.

"It's Zac," I confess.

"That married friend of Logan's?" Now my mom's eyes are bugging out and she has brought her hand up to clutch her throat in horror.

"He isn't married anymore. He got divorced while I was away. It's nice to know my parents think I'm either the slut that wouldn't know who her baby daddy is or, maybe worse, they think I'm a cheating homewrecker," I complain. I'm not really mad. I know my news has blindsided them.

"Oh stop it! You can't blame us for having questions," Momma D says in their defense. "What does Zac think about this new development?"

"Well..." I pick at the hem of my jacket, trying to decide how best to explain.

"Liv?" Mom asks, "Did you even tell him?"

"I'm working on it!" Every time I think of how to tell him, I freeze up.

"Oh, honey...you HAVE to tell him. Don't put it off. He deserves to know."

"I know! It's just that... Well, we aren't even really together. I mean obviously we *got together* but we aren't in a relationship or anything."

"Do you love him?" Mom asks softly.

"Yes...No! I don't know. Maybe? I'm so confused and this baby is just going to make a mess of everything."

"Babies have a way of changing things, no doubt, but that isn't necessarily bad. If you care for this man, then tell him. Give yourselves a chance to make something of it," Momma D advises. "Are you worried he won't want a baby?"

At that, I laugh. I guess that really would be the main concern for most women in my place but I'm actually concerned about the opposite problem. He'll want this baby more than he wants me.

"Zac loves kids. He wants a family more than just about anything. But how do I know if he is with me out of obligation or because he really wants a relationship? I don't want to just be a means to an end."

"Give him a chance. Be thankful he's a young man willing to be a father instead of running. My grandbaby deserves both parents. Don't push him away out of fear."

"Okay. I'll try, Mom. Do you know how much I love the both of you?"

"What's not to love?" asks Momma D.

Chapter Twenty-Two: Liv
News Flash! Life isn't Fair

"I'm so sorry, Liv!" she cries with tears running down her pale face.

Charli's eyes are swollen and bloodshot. I don't know if she's ever looked worse. Loving her like a sister almost my whole life, I've always known she has my back in every situation. I also know she's hurting right now in a way I can't really understand.

But how do I forgive this? She had no right.

"How could you do this to me, Charli?" I want to scream, throw things and say awful, hurtful things to her but all I can manage is quiet disappointment.

"Please," she sobs, "you have to forgive me."

I stand with my back to her and my eyes closed. "I'm trying."

"It's no excuse, I know that...but after you left I was so angry and hurt and confused. I wanted to hate you but I couldn't. I know you didn't plan this. This horribly cruel twist of fate has made me feel like I'm not a real woman. I keep thinking Logan deserves a wife that can give him babies. All his friends are fathers, or soon to be fathers, and he is being left out and it's my fault."

I turn back to face her. "Okay, but how does that excuse what you did to *me*?" I need to know why she did this. After Zac had called me - *yelled at me* - I'd left my parents and rushed home to confront Charli.

"It doesn't! I know that. But here I am feeling worthless and Logan calls, supposedly to check in. I know immediately that something is up and he's scared to tell me. He says that Scott and Kelly have been putting off their news because of me. They were worried how I would take it."

Now I'm curious. "Their news? What's wrong with Scott and Kelly?" I ask.

"She's pregnant again."

"Oh, Charli..." I know this must have been the final, crushing blow.

"Yeah," she says, "I didn't handle it well. Everyone deserves the right to be a parent, so I start thinking about Zac and how badly he wants a kid. Next thing I know, I'd called him." She flops down onto our couch and covers her face with both hands.

"It wasn't your place to tell him. This is between he and I, and you should have let me decide when and how he learned this."

"I know!"

She jumps up and comes over to where I'm still standing, right inside the doorway of our apartment. She isn't confident enough to try and touch me but I guess she's decided I won't actually kill her if she's within arm's reach.

"Zac is so mad at me," I tell her, "and he'll be here soon to talk

145

all this over."

"He will get over it. He cares for you and he'll love this baby."

"I know but I'm not ready to play house and be a Mommy and Daddy together. We aren't even dating!"

"He's a great guy, Liv. You lusted over him and wanted him so badly, even after you ran away for a year and a half. Now that he's free and you can have him, do you really want to let him go?"

"No. I don't. But even more than that, I don't want him to love me just because I'm giving him a child. I want him to love me, for me."

"Then give him that chance. How could he resist falling for you?" She gives me an impish grin.

"Are you kissing my ass to get me to forgive you?" I say it harshly but I feel a small smile threatening to emerge.

"If it's working, then yes. I love you, Liv. I'm here for you. I'm sorry for being such a complete bitch earlier but it won't happen again. If you don't want Zac at your side through this pregnancy, then I will be. I'll get ice cream at midnight, rub your back, put up with your mood swings and any other thing you need during this. I'll live vicariously through you, get to experience pregnancy by your side and be your slave for the next eight months. Then I'll be the best aunt possible to your little munchkin."

"I've heard that it's hard to shave after your belly gets big. Will you shave my legs?" I ask as I negotiate our terms for forgiveness.

"Yes, you lazy bitch, I will shave your legs for you *after* you get too big to do it yourself," she concedes.

"What about my hoo-hah? I don't want to deliver my baby with a giant bush blocking the door," I tell her. I even manage to keep a straight face.

"Don't press your luck!"

After coming to an agreement about her duties during this pregnancy, a little more crying, and even allowing her to give me a hug to seal the deal, Charli grabs her car keys to leave before Zac arrives. She's going to meet Logan for dinner to give us some privacy. I'd love some moral support but I know she's right. He and I will have a harder time negotiating than Charli and I did.

It isn't long before I hear heavy footsteps coming up the metal stairs and then a brisk pounding on my door. If his phone call hadn't been enough to tip me off to his current mood, I have no illusions now.

"Hey," I say softly as I pull the door toward me and motion him in.

"Hey? That's how you want to start this?" he asks. Instead of waiting for my reply, he walks into my living room like he owns the place, shoves both hands into his pockets and proceeds with his lecture.

"So, we have a mind blowing night of sex, we spend a month of phone calls and hot text messages, and then I get a brief call to say you need space. I thought I couldn't be any more pissed off... but I was wrong. Charli's phone call redefined my limits of fury. What in the hell were you thinking, Liv? Did you even plan on telling me you're pregnant?"

"Of course, I was! I wouldn't keep this from you!" I yell at him. I had promised myself I was going to be a rational adult and keep everything very civilized. That promise never had a chance.

"Really? I would like to think you'd tell me, as this baby's *father*...before you ran off and shared it with everyone!"

"I'm sorry!" I'm apologizing but it probably isn't coming across as genuine as I'd like it to. I hate being yelled at and I can't help but fight back. "I didn't post it online or take out a billboard. I told my best friend because I'm fucking freaked out!"

This finally gets through to him. He relaxes his shoulders, slumping down onto my couch.

"Liv...," he says quietly, leaning forward and resting his forehead on his hands in defeat. "I'm sorry I yelled at you. I know this was unexpected but..."

"Unexpected?" I laugh at his understatement.

"Come over here and sit with me?" he asks. I resist briefly but eventually join him. He leans back to put his arm around my shoulders. "We will figure this out."

"It's just too much, too soon. I'm not sure I can do this."

He stiffens. "Are you considering an abortion?" This thought is obviously horrifying him.

"No, I'm not."

He exhales in relief and I'm reminded how rare he is. *How many guys would want a girl they'd knocked up, after one night of sex, to keep the baby?*

"I believe a woman has the right to decide what's best for her," I say, "but that's just not an option I could consider. I won't put the baby up for adoption either."

"No! Absolutely not! If you can't keep this baby, then I'll take it!" he tells me instantly. My heart sinks.

I'm glad he loves children. I'm glad he wants this baby and to be a father but his words prove what I feared. I'm just not that important to him and I shouldn't be surprised. We haven't had the opportunity to build a relationship.

Right now, this baby comes first. It will be my first priority and obviously, it will be his. Any bond we try to make between us now will be because we are forcing it for the baby's sake. If we are truly meant to be together, it will need to come later and because it's something we both want.

"I'm not giving you our baby, Zac. I'm raising my child but I will never keep it from you or prevent you from being a full-time father. We will do this together."

"I'm so glad you feel that way," he says with a smile before leaning closer to kiss my temple. "I'd love it if you'd move into my place. I have an extra room that would be a great nursery and..."

"Whoa!" I pull away and stare at him in shock. "You expect me to move in with you?" *He has to be kidding!*

"Well, yeah. There isn't enough room here for me and the baby, besides Charli and Logan still live here too, so..."

"We aren't moving in together!" I screech, jumping up to start pacing in front of the couch.

"I know it's a lot quicker than expected but..."

"Zac, we will raise this baby together but I didn't say *we* would be together," I explain.

"But, I thought... I thought you wanted this."

"I want you but that doesn't mean we are in love and we should plan our happily ever after. Life isn't that easy. If I weren't pregnant, then we'd go on dates and have lots of hot sex. Maybe we'd fall for each other and make a serious commitment but we can't go into hyperdrive because of this baby. It wouldn't work out."

"We will make it work, damn it!" His voice is elevating again and he looks pissed.

"You just got divorced! I'm not going to be the replacement wife just because I'm giving you the kid you always wanted!"

"That isn't fair!" he growls. Now standing in front of me, he's glaring like I'm infuriating him. *I probably am.*

"News flash! Life ISN'T fair!"

"You are acting ridiculous about this. Why aren't you even willing to give us a try?" he asks.

"Because if it fails, that's worse for our child then if we just waited until we were ready."

"I am ready," he says.

"I'm not," I reply.

There's nothing else to say. He walks out of my home, slamming the door behind him.

Chapter Twenty-Three: Liv

Do They Hate Me Now?

"Oh my God! Does this ever end?"

Charli holds my hair back as I give in to my new morning ritual of vomiting within minutes of waking up.

"Well, according to the books, this should go away after the first trimester. So you only have about four more weeks. According to Kelly... all pregnancies are different and when she carried the twins, she had thrown up at least twice a day until delivery.

"This kid better be worth it! She has to win the Nobel prize or cure cancer or *something* because this sucks!" I complain before another wave of nausea shuts me up.

"This baby will be perfect," Charli assures me. "You know, Kelly says she feels great, hasn't had a single day of sickness. She's convinced this one will be a boy since it's so different than what she went through with the girls."

"Good for her," I say bitterly.

I've spent the last month having to pee every ten minutes, so exhausted I'm practically useless at work and puking every morning almost as soon as I crawl out of bed. And even though I'm barely pregnant, my clothes are already feeling snug and I've gained seven pounds. I feel like a whale, or a hippopotamus, or the baby of a whale and a hippopotamus.

"Hey, girls, I..." Logan, poking his head into the bathroom, gets one look at what's going on and bails like the man he is. "Nevermind!" we hear as he disappears.

He's trying to be patient with the chaos our lives have become but with Charli still overly emotional from her hormone injections and me puking, peeing and bitching all the time, the guy is a frazzled mess.

After the worst of the digestive assault fades, Charli brings me a glass of ginger ale. I have always hated ginger ale, so of course now, it's the only thing I want to drink. I'm also eating my weight in lemon drops.

Yeah, surely I'm a candidate for "Mom of the Year" right? Doesn't every pregnancy expert tell you soda and candy are just what your growing fetus needs?

"Oh my God! What is that smell?" I inhale deeply. I've been extremely oversensitive to scents and we've had to change laundry soap, throw out all scented candles and ban anything with garlic.

"Sorry! I'll stop him!" Charli jumps up to run toward the kitchen but I manage to grab the hem of her shirt in time to stop her.

"No! It smells like heaven." I close my eyes to focus and better enjoy the smell.

"Now I know you've been taken over by the Pod People. Liv... the smell is coffee. You hate coffee. You hate the taste and smell of anything derived from the coffee bean. I told Logan to grab Starbucks on his way to the office but he must have forgotten."

"Well, my little parasite must love coffee. I'm about to go bury my nose in the bag of grounds for her."

"Her? We still don't know if she's...I mean, if 'it' is a girl or boy. I don't want you to be disappointed."

"She's a girl," I assert. "I just know."

"But what if..." Charli insistently starts as I shake my head and refuse to listen.

I know my baby is a girl. I can tell. *Shouldn't a mother be able to intuit these things?*

"Look," I tell her, "She is a girl. She has to be a girl. The thought of having to deal with outdoor plumbing totally freaks me the fuck out. I know how to take care of a *man's* pipe but what do I do with a tiny little hose? How can I change a boy's diaper and have to move that thing around to clean him up? I can't touch a baby one! It's just weird. It's just wrong."

"Seriously?" she asks derisively. She's shaking her head as she leaves to join Logan.

To hell with her! I know I'm right!

Thirty minutes later, with my nausea on temporary hiatus, I'm dressed and ready to go. By dressed, I mean wearing leggings and an oversized tunic. This is now my "go to" ensemble.

Sitting on our couch with a giant mug of steaming coffee, I take a deep breath and enjoy the dark, rich scent. I know better than drink it - it's on my "No-No" list from the obstetrician - and it would probably still taste awful to me but the aroma is intoxicating. I can't put it down so I let my willing slave answer the knock at our door.

"Hey, Zac. Come on in," Charli says before giving him a quick hug.

"Thanks. Where's Logan?" Zac looks around the room, avoiding eye contact with me.

"I'm here," Logan says, walking out of his room and grabbing his jacket from the hook near the door, "but Charli and I are leaving to go see my folks. Glad I got to see you first, though, man."

They shake hands and smile. I feel bad that I'm the reason they don't see each other as often as they'd like.

"Tell them hello for me," Zac requests.

"Absolutely!" Logan promises and then he and Charli leave us... alone.

Seeing him is hard and I still feel that magnetic pull. I want to jump up, even though it's getting difficult to jump anywhere nowadays, and run my hands over his broad shoulders and muscled abs. I want to pull him into my bedroom and get naked. It takes all my strength to act like he's just a friend. *He is my Baby Daddy, so maybe friend isn't exactly accurate?*

"Hi," I begin, with a nice, big smile. I'm playing nice so hopefully, he will too.

"Hi," he says and although he smiles back at me, it's different. His smile used to be warm and inviting. It made me want to cuddle up and talk all night. It also made me want to do very naughty things until we passed out from exhaustion. Now he's holding back and the smile never reaches those dark chocolate eyes of his that have always made my stomach flutter.

Of course, now those flutters might be gas. That's been a majorly embarrassing issue lately.

"Thank you for doing this," he says.

"I'm happy to see your parents, especially Mikey again," I tell him, "but do they hate me now?"

His head jerks up in shock and he frowns at me. "Why would you think they hate you? Liv, you already know they like you.

Mikey practically worships you. He's been on countdown all week until you could come visit him."

"I didn't mean Mikey. I meant your mom and dad. How are Ginger and James handling this?" It literally hurts to think they dislike me now.

"They are excited at the thought of a grandbaby. It will be fine," he assures me.

I have my doubts but try to trust him as we head out of the apartment and down to his car. Zac had explained our situation to them weeks ago but when he'd asked me to go with him for a visit, I'd been reluctant.

Hi, Mr. and Mrs. Reynolds. Remember me? I'm the girl that was hot for your son even when he was still married. I'm the one that slept with him the same night I got home from an eighteen-month absence and got knocked up because I'm too stupid to remember antibiotics can mess up birth control pills. I don't want to marry him, move in with him, or even date him... but having wild animal sex with him is still very appealing. Aren't you excited I'm the mother of your grandchild?

Yep. This should go smoothly.

"Liv," his voice cuts into my worries and I can hear the lecture in his tone. "I told you. You have nothing to worry about."

"Uh huh." *This man is deluding himself.*

The drive takes a couple of hours and we pass it with small talk and companionable slices of silence. We carefully avoid anything that touches too close to our opposing views on the baby.

He swings the car into a wide driveway in front of an older, ranch style home and shifts into park but we continue to sit quietly in the car. I'm trying hard to grow a pair and open the door but the sanctuary of the vehicle has too tight a hold on me.

"So..." I whisper.

"So," he responds before sliding his hand across the seat to intertwine our fingers. Still facing forward, he gives them a reassuring squeeze.

The contact of his skin, even this tiny amount, has my heart rate picking up and my bones liquefying. I repeatedly swallow and take a deep breath, in need of more oxygen.

"Liv, can we just..."

In my hyper-emotional state, I'm afraid to let him go on. I'm trying to stay strong and follow through with my decision but when he's near I feel my resolve cracking and crumbling at the edges.

It's our little parasite's fault. She's flooding me with all these girly hormones and I'm crying at the most ridiculous things, even commercials. Charli caught me sobbing and worrying about the husband in an insurance ad on television.

The poor guy was on the phone with Jake from State Farm, but his wife was convinced he'd called a phone sex girl. What if she leaves him and breaks up their family over a misunderstanding?

I am so messed up.

"I'm ready. Let's go!" I say with an enthusiasm I don't feel. Taking back my hand, I climb out of his car.

It's time to man up, and do this.

Chapter Twenty-Four: Zac

I've Changed My Mind!

"Mom, Dad?" I yell through the front door as we enter. "We're here!"

A blur of motion, also known as my little brother, is on a collision course with Liv and I have mere seconds to save her.

"Ugh," I groan after jumping in front of her and going down with Mikey. He's just had his sixteenth birthday, grown several inches over the summer, and has filled out enough to do some serious damage if he tried. He might be forever stuck as a young child in his mind and heart but his body is almost that of a grown man.

"Zac!" He hugs me from our sprawled positions on the floor and then struggles to get away from me in order to reach Liv.

"Hi, Mikey!" Liv says excitedly and when her face softens like it always does around my brother, my heart tightens and gives a heavy thump. Gone is the mask of indifference and the cautious weighing of words. She is once again my Liv, the ferociously beautiful and sexy woman I'd fallen for, the woman now carrying my child, and the woman that doesn't want me anymore.

"Be careful with Liv, okay buddy? You can't be so rough." I watch Mikey as she reaches up on her tiptoes to kiss his cheek and wrap her arm around his waist. He is ecstatic and practically bouncing to contain his joy but his touch is gentle and I relax.

"I'll be careful. I won't hurt her," he promises.

"I know you won't," she assures him but I can't help reminding him one more time that he forgets how strong he is now.

We follow him out of the entryway and into the living room, where my parents are waiting. They're smiling but I see the tense postures and tight expressions. Liv notices too and her face falls.

"Hello, Mr. and Mrs. Reynolds. How are you?" she asks in a timid voice that doesn't fit with the Liv I know.

"Good. We're good," my dad says.

"But honey, how are you?" Mom asks, as she pulls away from Dad and approaches Liv cautiously. "Are you feeling okay?"

"Oh, yes ma'am. I guess so, for the most part."

"I'm glad. Those first few months can be just awful. I was sick with Zac for the entire nine and a half months," Mom says and I know she is really trying but I see her hands fidget with her necklace and adjust her blouse enough times to know she's nervous.

"Nine and a half months!" This news has startled Liv out of her polite coma and my mom laughs. Then they both laugh and the mood of the room lightens considerably.

"Yes, he was due the first of February but two weeks later he was still snug and tight with no plans of coming to meet us. It was a Friday, I had a doctor's appointment and I was getting worried. I was also sick and tired of being the size of a house!

158

They said we would induce labor on Monday but as usual, our Zac had his own plans. Saturday night, right before midnight, my water broke. We rushed off to the hospital and he was born that next evening." She smiles in my direction and I smile back, a little embarrassed for Liv to hear this story. The tale of your birth isn't exactly manly.

"Nine and a half months..." Liv trails off as she sinks down onto the couch. My mom joins her, putting an arm around her shoulder. Dad, Mikey, and I just stand around like we have no clue what to do with ourselves. Which of course, we don't.

"Yes, but he was worth it. The minute I saw my ten-pound, little man, I'd felt an instant love that's indescribable," Mom tells her.

"Zac weighed ten pounds! Oh, hell no!" Liv jumps up and starts pacing frantically. "I've changed my mind! I can't do this."

"Liv, honey," Mom croons, expertly coaxing her back to the couch, "Everything will be fine. All babies are different. Mikey only weighed nine pounds."

"Mom," I warn, as Liv goes pale and groans. "I don't think that's helping."

"We're fine, Zachary. You just go visit with your father and brother and let us girls talk a bit more."

I'm reluctant to leave them but eventually, I walk over to the other side of the room so Mikey can show me the puzzle he just completed and answer some questions Dad has about my res-taurant. I sneak glances at the women periodically and strain to hear as much of their conversation as possible.

When I hear Liv ask Mom if she hates her now, I stand stock still, barely breathing, and listen for my mom's response.

"Of course not!" she assures. "James and I are just thrilled to know our first grandchild will have you as a mother. We all adore you, dear."

"Oh," Liv snuffles. "It's just...Well, I thought you'd be mad because I can't... I mean, because we aren't... Zac and I just..."

My very traditional but supportive mother embraces her warmly, plants a kiss on top of that outrageously red hair and laughs.

"I'd be lying if I said I'm not hoping the two of you manage to work this out. Nothing would make me happier than seeing my son with someone he cares so much about. I see how he is with you. You are important to him and I think you have similar feelings for him. But whether you decide to be together or not, you are the mother of my grandbaby and that makes you family. Understand?"

"Yes. Thank you. No matter what happens, all of you are special to me and I'm so thankful my daughter will have you as her grandparents."

"Daughter!" I boom as I take the five large strides it takes me to be back at her side. "We're having a daughter? How do you know? You promised I could go to the ultrasound! Isn't it too early? Is it some new test?"

"Breathe, Zac!" Liv is laughing at me like she finds all this extremely funny.

I'm tired of her keeping things from me. She should have told me we're having a girl! "You promised to keep me informed!" I accuse. I'm trying not to lose my temper in front of my family but she makes it so damn difficult.

"I didn't have any tests to confirm it but I feel like she's a girl," she explains as she looks down and places a protective hand over her abdomen.

I start to relax. "So...you don't know? You just think it's a she?" I need to make sure this is perfectly clear.

She rubs her belly softly, even though I can't detect a bulge yet, and smiles.

"Call it mother's intuition," she insists.

"Well, I wouldn't start painting the nursery pink just yet..." my dad interjects. "Ginger was convinced Mikey was a girl too."

"Mikey is NOT a girl!" my little brother yells in disgust.

"No, of course not. We all know you are a boy," Liv tells him.

"And Liv has a big boy in her tummy too. Mommy told me you are going to have a baby and then I will be the uncle and I will get to play with him," he says assuredly.

"Mikey, it might be a girl," I tell him. "We don't know yet."

"I know, Zac! I know it. Mikey knows that Liv's baby is a baby boy. I get to show him how to draw pictures and build with Legos and throw a ball. He will be my friend."

"Maybe you're right. We will have to wait and see," I tell him but he isn't buying it. My brother redefines stubborn.

"Do you get to be his uncle too, Zac? Are you Liv's baby's uncle like I am?" he asks me hopefully.

Uh oh. I thought my parents had explained this better. "Ummm...no. I'm the Daddy. You are the only uncle," I explain.

"You are Liv's baby's Daddy?" he asks in confusion.

Damn, he just referred to me as the "Baby Daddy." My dad is cracking up, my mom is hiding a smile behind her hand and Liv is rolling her eyes.

"I'm the Mommy and Zac is the Daddy," Liv tells Mikey but he looks even more confused.

"Well..." he pauses to think, "Why didn't you invite me?"

"WHAT!" I yell and everyone jumps a little. *Is he asking why he wasn't at the baby's conception? For fuck's sake, what has my mother been telling him?*

"Zac...Why didn't I get to come to your wedding to Liv?"

161

Mikey asks innocently and I feel like a complete jackass.

"Oh, Mikey," Liv says as she stands up and takes his hand in hers. "We didn't get married. We would never have a wedding without you!"

"But..." He shakes his head, "Mommy said when people fall in love they get married and then they can be a mommy and daddy when the baby grows in her tummy. If you didn't get married, then how did that baby get in Liv's tummy, Zac?"

The whole room is silent. I'm not getting help from anyone.

"Hey Mikey, how about we take you to your favorite park? We can even get some ice cream!" I promise.

"But, Zac..." he starts.

"Grab your coat, kid!" I cut in, as I try herding him out the door.

Chapter Twenty-Five: Liv
I Miss Pooping

"I miss pooping."

"Shut up, Liv," Kyle moans.

"Well, I do! My spawn makes me constipated!" I say. My greatest joy in life right now is making Kyle, Ronan, or both uncomfortable enough to run from me. It is all kinds of awesome.

"And my boobs are so sensitive."

"Damn it, Liv! If you don't shut up, I'm going to fire you!" Ronan promises from behind the bar.

"So... you guys don't want to hear about my mucus plug? Because I read that when I get close to time for labor..."

"I'm out!" Kyle can't get past me, so he vaults over the top of the bar to escape. Ronan is still trapped and looking desperate.

"Olivia Marie Garrett," Charli barks, "You stop tormenting those guys right now! Let them finish the stocking. Kelly will be here any minute to pick us up, so go grab your purse."

"Oh, you're no fun," I complain but I do as she asks and leave the boys alone...for now.

Kelly, Charli and I are going to go shopping this afternoon for baby stuff. I'm a little jealous because Kelly had her ultrasound this morning. She'll have found out the baby's sex by now so she can start picking out bedding and clothing and all that other good stuff while I still have a couple more weeks until I'll know. Scott wants a boy so badly. He loves his twin daughters of course but according to his wife, he dreams of all things blue, little league games, and not being so outnumbered by the females in his family. I reminded him that girls can like blue and play any sport boys can but nothing short of having a son, will help the gender balance.

For myself, I've tried to be good and purchase gender neutral things so far. *It's possible I might have slipped up a little and bought that pink ruffled bloomer set with the matching headband but I think I've shown a lot of restraint, all things considered.*

As soon as I get my ultrasound confirmation, the gallon of lavender paint I hid in the bar's storeroom will go up on the walls. Thanks to Ronan's surprise, I now have a nursery. I smile, remembering how he tried to blow off his generosity.

"You did this?" I asked him in shock, when I came home from a weeklong trip, shooting a music festival for a new arts and entertainment magazine. Ronan had hired a contractor to add another room in the apartment, right next to mine.

"It adds value to the place to have another room," Ronan had insisted as I spun in circles, admiring the new space.

"You already let us have it for way less than you could be charging for a loft of this size," I reminded him.

"Shut up before I remember that and up the rent then," he grumbled as he walked out the door to return to his bar downstairs.

Being the emotional wreck I am right now, I had sat down in the middle of the newly partitioned room, connected to mine by a set of French doors, and cried.

I'm so over all this crying shit!

"Charli, where's Logan?" Kelly asks as she enters the bar, without even a hello for anyone. She looks hurried and her lips are pinched.

"Oh, hey Kelly...he had to run up to work to help Dana with some paperwork. Why? What's up?" Charli asks with concern.

"Oh, I just think Scott needs some "dude time." He's kind of freaking out."

"Why?" we both ask her in unison.

"Well..." she drops the scowl and beams before rubbing her rounded abdomen. "We are having another girl!"

"Congratulations!" Charli screams, running over to give her a hug.

"That's great! Now my Scarlett will have a best friend," I tell her.

"Scarlett?" Charli asks.

"Yes," I tell them, "I finally decided on a name. I'm sure she'll be a redhead like me, so I've decided to call her Scarlett. I had originally wanted her middle name to be after you, Charli... but Scarlett Charlotte sucks. If I knew for sure she was going to grow up to be a superhero, then it would rock but... So, I'm sorry, but I'm going to have to go with Michaela, for Mikey. I can't wait to tell him!" I rub my hands together in anticipation.

"Ummm...I wouldn't run off and get his hopes up just yet, Liv. You know, it is possible you are having a boy," Charli warns.

"I did think I was having a boy, you know," Kelly reminds us. "So mother's intuition can be wrong,"

"Yeah, I suppose it's possible... but doubtful. I'm having a little flame-haired Scarlett Michaela Garrett."

"Garrett? Not Reynolds? Won't that hurt Zac's feelings? Have you discussed names with him?" Kelly asks.

Shit. It had never occurred to me. Zac might like some input into his daughter's name. He'll probably prefer she be a Reynolds but I hate the idea of my own child having a different last name than mine. *Damn, this "Baby Daddy" stuff is complicated!*

"I'll talk to him," I say before changing the subject. "Let's get going! I need to find some pants that will actually button. My work shirt looks awful with leggings."

With sighs of relief from both Ronan and Kyle, we leave for the outdoor shopping mall downtown. In no time at all, Kelly finds crib bedding in hot pink with lime green polka dots. She also buys an ivory lace gown as a "coming home" outfit but doesn't need much else since she kept all the twins' baby stuff.

I manage to find some halfway decent jeans. Granted, if you pull up my shirt to see them in their entirety, you'll probably laugh your ass off. There's a big stretchy panel that goes all the way up to the underside of my boobs. They are scary ugly at the waistband but undeniably comfortable. I'm thinking the most terrifying change during my pregnancy is my willingness to give up my shit hot style in favor of comfort.

It had better not be a permanent change! I will not be that mom with no makeup, baggy jeans, and driving a fucking mini-van.

We are wandering around the maternity clothing store when I notice Charli has strayed away from us. Leaving Kelly looking at nursing bras that are so complicated you need an instruction manual to figure out how to use them, I scan the aisles for Charli. I find my best friend near the back of the store, sitting on a wooden bench near the dressing rooms, clutching a small round pillow.

"Hey," I say, sliding down next to her and bumping her hip over to give my ever-expanding ass a little more room. "You okay?"

"I'm fine," she whispers but her voice sounds choked and she won't make eye contact.

"You are lying bitch," I whisper back as I slide my arm around her narrow shoulders. "Tell me what's going on, Charli."

"I'm just... It's nothing. Sorry." She stands up, drops the pillow to the bench, and leaves me for the direction we left Kelly.

She looks defeated and I feel helpless. I reach over and grab the little pillow. When I look more closely, I notice it has two thin elastic bands dangling from the underside. *What the hell kind of pillow is this?*

"Do you need a dressing room?" an overly friendly sales girl in tight pants and a fitted sweater asks. I instantly hate her, solely based on the fact she is rocking that outfit and I'm looking at clothes that would work as a circus tent.

"No. I'm good. Thanks, though."

"We have different sizes of bumps if you need one," she says, but I have no clue what she's talking about.

"Huh?"

She points at the pillow I'm holding. "The belly bump pillow? We have different sizes if you want to try on clothing to see what it will look like when you are farther along. I'd guess you still have several months to go, so it is always a good idea to tie a belly bump pillow on when choosing clothes to make sure you still have room to grow."

"Shit!" I shake my head in understanding.

"Excuse me?" The girl looks offended.

"Nothing. Sorry. I've got to go." I throw the pillow in her direction and go looking for Charli.

She has been doing so well. At least, I thought she was. Since our mess over finding out I was pregnant, she's been by my side and supportive through everything I've dealt with and never once acted upset or mad. Realistically I know it wasn't easy for her but I believed she was coping well. *Have I been deluding myself?*

"Charli?" I find her near the pajama rack and pull her toward me. Wrapping my arms tightly around her, in an emotional and uncharacteristic hug, I start to cry. *Damn these pregnancy hormones!*

"I'm fine, Liv," she says into my hair but she's holding me just as tightly. "I will be fine. I'm sorry to worry you."

"Stop that! I'm here for you. You don't have to be brave and strong all the damn time!"

"Okay," she chuckles. "I really am fine. I just saw the pillow thing and wondered what it would look like if I were…"

"If you looked like you swallowed a watermelon, whole?" I ask and she laughs again.

"Maybe," she admits.

"Don't give up!" I demand.

"I won't," she promises.

"Okay, good." I pull back and wipe my tears and disgusting runny nose on a napkin I find in my purse. I know better than go anywhere without tissues or napkins now.

"Let's go help Kelly pick out a bra," she suggests.

"She swears my boobs are going to get even bigger after I give birth and my milk comes in," I tell her. "You may have to walk around with me to help hold them up at that point. My back hurts now from lugging these girls around."

"Let Zac do it! He'd love to help you out…" She is really laughing now. I'm glad she's feeling better but does it have to be at my

168

expense?

"Shut the hell up," I respond but I'm smiling.

After paying for our purchases, we decide to take a break for lunch. I'm always either nauseated and convinced food is the devil or starving so badly I'd be willing to eat anything I can get my hands on. Heading toward the small Italian café we love, I'm stopped by the delicious aroma of freshly brewed coffee. It smells even better than the kind Logan brews at home. *This is so messed up!*

"There she goes again," Charli says, shaking her head in amused exasperation.

"I just need to inhale it a few more minutes..."

"Well, I need to eat! This baby girl is starving, so let's go!" Kelly demands.

"You two go get a table," I suggest, "I'm going to just pop into that little coffee shop for a couple of minutes, get me a fix, and then I'll meet up with you."

"You shouldn't be drinking coffee," Kelly says.

"I'm not! I'm just going to wander around in there like a dazed junkie on a high, enjoying the smell of everyone else's cups of heaven."

"Yeah...because that won't look crazy..." Charli laughs.

"Growing a human is crazy," I assure her as I push her in the direction of the café. "Get us a table. I'll be there in two minutes... five minutes, tops!"

"Uh huh." She sounds doubtful.

Screw her. I need this.

I push open the heavy door and step into the cozy interior filled with dark wood tables and chairs, cushioned couches and ottomans in small clusters, and a long granite counter where God's angels are preparing the nectar of Heaven. I close my eyes

169

and just enjoy it.

"Excuse me," I hear a masculine voice say as I'm bumped from behind in some guy's hurry to get in line. I want to get pissed but if I'm being fair, I am the one that stopped and blocked the traffic near the door.

With my eyes now open, I look around and smile in contentment. My contentment ends abruptly when I see *them*. Even with his back to me, I know it's Zac. I know that thick dark hair and even the small freckle on the back of his neck. I know that tall, lean body and broad shoulders. As I watch his long-fingered hand lift a mug of steaming coffee to his mouth, I remember those expert fingers touching every inch of my body.

But who in the fuck is he with?

Across from him, sitting on the edge of her seat and clutching a small cup between her delicate hands, is a gorgeous blonde. And she is laughing. *What the hell?*

I feel my muscles tense and a furious heat fills me. He's been calling to check on me every day. I get numerous texts where he swears he can't stop thinking about me. He wants me to give us a real chance and thinks we can make this work. He's been wearing me down and I've been considering agreeing.

And now, here he sits on a date with another woman. Here he is, with a thin and beautiful blonde while I can't button my pants because I'm incubating his child.

Hell no.

I paste a huge smile on my bitter face and stride with purpose to the small, intimate grouping of chairs they had chosen. I see her notice me first. She smiles slightly but looks confused as it becomes apparent I'm heading right for her.

Then he sees me and I watch his initial smile turn to panic.

"Hi," I say loud and cheerfully as I stick my hand out toward the blonde. He's right to look concerned over my friendliness.

"Uh...hello?" Her voice sounds sweet and hesitant as she extends her hand to receive my greeting.

Poor girl, she probably has no clue about the mess she's landed herself into.

"Liv..." Zac's voice has a warning in it but I don't care. He's not in charge.

"Yes, that's right. I'm Liv," I tell her. "I'm carrying his child." I rub my small, rounded tummy for emphasis. "What are you doing for him?"

Her face goes ghostly pale and her hands are shaking so badly she has to set the cup down on the nearby table. "Oh..." she breathes out softly. "Ummm...I'm not sure what you...I mean, I'm just..."

"You are just the hot girl he's trying to bang since I won't fuck him right now?" I ask as I watch two red spots of color appear on her cheeks.

"Liv!" Zac stands up and roughly grabs my arm to pull me away.

"So nice to meet you!" I call over my shoulder as he hauls me out of the coffee shop and away from her.

"What the hell is wrong with you!" he demands and I see his fury but it doesn't slow me down. I'm the one with the right to be furious.

"What's wrong with me? I'm not out on a date with some hot stud while trying to convince you we should be together. I'm not jumping the first available guy, even though this pregnancy is making me so damn horny all the time I get turned on when the breeze switches directions. I'm not..." But I can't say anything else because my traitorous tear ducts have struck again. *Damn hormones.* My rage has become wracking sobs and I don't even put up a fight when he pulls me against his strong chest and begins stroking my hair.

"Oh, baby..." he croons.

"No!" I snuffle out. "You don't get to call me that, asshole."

I'm hoping for remorse or even a little more anger. Instead, he chuckles. "Liv, I'm not on a date."

"Yes, you are! I saw her! And she's beautiful and blonde and still has a waist!"

He kisses the top of my head and squeezes me even tighter. "You are beautiful. You've always been the most beautiful woman I've ever known and now while carrying my child, your beauty almost brings me to my knees. Liv, I'm NOT on a date."

"But..."

"No! That was Tiffany, she's a..."

"Oh, she looks like a Tiffany...a perfect little..."

"Shut the hell up and listen to me," he demands. I'm feeling generous, so I comply. "Tiffany is the real estate agent that helped me find the restaurant. I ran into her while she was waiting for her *husband* to meet her on his lunch break. I was out here to get this." He hands me a small wrapped box with a large silk bow tied on top.

"Oh," I say meekly, "Her husband?"

"Yes," he confirms while tucking a stray strand of my hair behind my ear.

"Maybe I should go apologize to Tiffany?" I suggest.

"I'd say she deserves at least that but open the box first."

I pull on the ribbon and slide the lid open. Inside is a small silver rattle with "Reynolds" engraved on it. It's beautiful and I love it. It also makes me realize we better have that name talk pretty soon.

"Thank you. It's great. I love it." I tell him as I clutch the tiny thing to my chest.

"I'm glad. There isn't anything I won't do for this baby, Liv. I hope you know that."

My heart sinks. I should be thrilled that he wants this child so much but once again his words have made me realize a truth. He loves and wants this child. He will do anything for this baby, including committing himself to me.

Can I be with a man when I will forever doubt if I was his first choice or just the best choice for his child's sake?

Chapter Twenty-Six: Zac
Yeah, He Needs To Die

"You're beautiful," I tell her.

"Blah blah blah...hand me another lemon drop before I puke."

Liv snatches the piece of candy from me before I have time to hand it to her. Popping it into her mouth, she falls down onto her low couch with her eyes closed and brow furrowed. I feel awful that she's still having so much nausea.

I'd arrived a little earlier than necessary this morning, hoping we could talk before the doctor's appointment. Instead, I have fetched ginger ale with no ice, doled out lemon drops from her giant stash in the basket on the coffee table, and tried to be sympathetic as she moans.

"You know," she starts, "I used to complain about cramps and bleeding every month but, at least, I didn't feel like puking every morning and I wasn't fat."

"You aren't fat," I assure her as I sit down on the floor next to the couch and reach over to smooth her hair away from her forehead.

"I'm pretty sure I'm visible from outer space."

I try to keep my laugh in. I don't want to disregard how she feels but she is far from fat. Her belly has a nice roundness now but it's sexy as hell. And her breasts are even more spectacular than before, which I'd thought was impossible. She's still slender everywhere else and her amped up curves are so damn distracting that I usually lose my train of thought when I look at her.

"Can I get you anything else?" I ask her.

"No, I'll be fine in a few minutes. It usually doesn't last too long."

"I'm sorry. It's my fault," I whisper into her ear before placing a single kiss on her temple. I watch her lips form a small smile and I'm encouraged.

"Yes, yes it is. You knocked me up all by yourself. I had nothing to do with it," she mocks.

"Well, how could I help myself? No one could have resisted. Do you know what you do to me, Liv?"

She turns her face toward me, opens her eyes, and smiles mischievously. "What, Zac? Tell me exactly what I do to you."

I groan and adjust the way I'm sitting. Even though we'd cleared up the confusion at the coffee shop and we've been talking daily, I've felt a distance growing between us. I feel like she's been pulling away from me. But now, stretched out on the couch with heavily lidded eyes and biting at her full bottom lip, I can feel how much she wants me.

Hadn't she mentioned pregnancy was making her horny?

"Liv..." I reach out, run my index finger over her bottom lip and hear her breath catch. Afraid of being rejected, but unable to help myself, I lean in closer and kiss her.

175

The electricity races between us with the contact and she opens her mouth to mine. The feel of her tongue darting between my lips makes my heart start hammering in my chest like a jackhammer and I feel the hot tension of excitement as a certain body part realizes he might get a little action for a change.

I move one hand up to cup her cheek, trying to move slowly, but she grabs my wrist and guides my hand to one of her full, hot breasts and I almost lose it on the spot. She's pushing up against my hand as I knead the fullness and start exploring this glorious body I've missed more than I believed possible.

My hand moves to the other breast and then down to feel the round firmness of her belly. It's the first time she's let me touch her and knowing my child is growing inside her, right under where my hand now rests, has me in awe. I've managed to move so that I'm on my knees now, still at the side of the couch but above her, without putting any weight on her. I kiss down her neck and onto her collarbone. She starts to unbutton her shirt, and I'm trying hard not to start jumping up and down in victory when all of sudden she goes completely still.

"Liv?" I groan out hoarsely, "What's…"

"Shut up!" she commands as she closes her eyes and lays both hands on her belly in concentration.

"Is something wrong?" I'm starting to panic. Is she hurting? Does something feel wrong with the baby?

"Oh…" is all she says as a smile spreads across her face and her eyes fill with tears.

"Liv, honey, what is it?" She is absolutely radiant.

"It's the…I mean, I think…" She wrinkles her forehead for a minute and then smiles again. "I feel her! Zac, she's moving and I can feel her!"

I fall back to a sitting position and just watch her as she pulls her shirt up and softly runs her hands over the skin of her abdomen. She's closed her eyes again and her expression is like one you'd see in a Renaissance painting of the Madonna and child. She is pure bliss.

"What does it feel like?" I whisper reverently.

"Ummm..." She thinks before answering, "It's like tiny little bubbles. It feels like when you take a bubble bath and the little foamy soap bubbles at the edges of the tub burst against your skin, except it's under my skin. It's like the way champagne tickles your nose right before you take that first sip."

I can see her radiant happiness and it fills me with joy. I'm also a little jealous that I can't feel the movement but it still seems like a miracle.

I lean forward, slide one of her hands away and place a little kiss right beside her navel. When I lay my cheek against her belly, she runs her fingers lightly through my hair and I never want this moment to end.

"Hey, guys?" Charli's voice interrupts our moment as she walks out of her and Logan's bedroom, yawning and stretching.

"What?" Liv asks, still completely calm and peaceful.

"Aren't you going to be late for your appointment?" Charli asks.

"Shit!" Liv and I say in unison as we finally get up and start scrambling for our stuff.

We've been waiting for this appointment, counting down the days, and now we will probably be late. They had better not bump us from the schedule or they will be dealing with a seriously pissed off Daddy-to-be. The Mommy will probably be even more difficult to deal with.

Within five minutes we are on the road, heading for the Women's Center and our appointment with Liv's obstetrician.

We were exactly seven minutes late. The receptionist sighs with aggravation when we sign in but one look from Liv convinces her to keep her thoughts to herself. She then has a nurse show us to a small, exam room.

"Dr. Willingham will be in shortly," the nurse says after weighing her and taking her blood pressure. She writes the results in Liv's chart and then leaves, closing the door behind her.

"So..." I say, unsure what to talk about as I look around at all the posters of lady business. It's all very intimidating. I'm surrounding by images of breasts and vaginas. You might think, as a man, I'd enjoy the artwork. *You'd be wrong*. These are not like the shit you see in Playboy spreads. This is the stuff of nightmares, making the female equipment I usually love, look foreign and complicated.

"Are you freaking out?" Liv asks with a knowing smirk.

"Nope."

"Liar."

"Whatever..." I can't look at her smile and arched eyebrow, and I can't look at all the medical posters any longer either, so I opt for staring at my shoes.

"If you think you're uncomfortable now, you should come to a regular visit," she tells me. "Imagine me in a paper gown, my feet up in metal stirrups and a doctor with latex gloves inserting torture devices into my vajayjay while he..."

"Stop! I've had enough!" I beg, "It sounds like a scene from a bad alien abduction movie!"

"Yeah, that's pretty accurate actually," she laughs. Then she turns to flash a dazzling smile toward the doorway as I hear the doctor entering.

"Hey, Liv!" says a friendly, deep voice.

"Hey, Dr. Will. How's it going?"

I turn, expecting an older gentleman with gray, thinning hair and a lined face with years of experience. Instead, I see a guy that's maybe thirty-five at most with all his hair, no gray, and deep dimples as he hugs the woman carrying my child.

He can't be the doctor! He looks like the actors you see on TV in those medical dramas and soap operas. What the hell?

"I'm good, Liv. Already delivered twins this morning and I have a mom in early labor right now, so it's an exciting day. How are you feeling?" His handsome face shows concern as he rests his hand on her shoulder.

I feel like punching him. Providing a black eye and maybe a broken nose would make me feel a little better about this whole situation.

"Not too bad," she answers as she looks up through her fringe of dark lashes.

Is she flirting? Yeah, he needs to die.

"Still nauseated?" Dr. 'Can't Keep His Hands to Himself' asks.

"Just in the morning. I can handle it," Liv tells him.

"I know you can. You're a tough cookie," he assures her with a wink.

I've had enough. "I'm Zac," I say loudly while stepping between them. "You know, the guy that impregnated her."

"Congratulations," he says.

Is he being sarcastic? Is he congratulating me for having had the opportunity to have sex with her? What the hell?

Liv starts to laugh and pushes on my shoulder. Of course, she would find this funny.

"Congratulations on becoming a new father is what I meant of course," the doctor adds but from the amusement on his face I'm sure he knows exactly how his words were taken. *What a prick.*

"So Liv, let's get you up on the table now." Dr. Dickhead says as I watch him gently take the arm of the woman carrying my child and help her slide onto the exam table.

I hate this guy.

I'm trying not to think of how many times this guy has looked at, and touched, the most intimate parts of her in the last several months. He's been getting to handle the parts she's been keeping from me. Hell, he's actually seen them more times than I have and that seems utterly wrong.

The nurse rejoins us. She dims the lights and wheels in a large monitor with tons of dials and knobs and a cord with some type of rectangular attachment. She tells Liv to relax back and lift her shirt. She then pulls the elastic waist of Liv's stretchy pants down low enough to make me swallow hard. Another inch or two and I'd get a view of the real deal. Tucking a large paper towel into the waistband and pulling it down to protect her pants, the nurse then grabs a big squeeze tube of lube.

What the fuck goes on in this doctor's office?

Dr. Asshole has now scrubbed his hands and put on gloves. He takes the lube and squeezes a large amount onto Liv's exposed belly.

"Shit! That's freezing!" Liv yelps and the doctor laughs.

"I know. Sorry. It will warm up some with the contact of your body heat. Be patient," he says with yet another wink.

I feel sick.

Doctor Douchebag takes the corded attachment and firmly presses into the gelatinous pile of goo on Liv's belly and slides it around while watching the monitor. Soon the machine comes to life and I hear a rhythmic whooshing noise.

"Oh, Zac," Liv says as she smiles over in my direction, finally acknowledging I'm part of this too, "Do you hear that?"

Ignoring my aggravation with the doctor, I pay attention to the black and white screen and listen as the strange sounds fill the room.

"Is that...Is that the baby's heartbeat?" I ask. There is strong, fast beat inside the waves of noise and I feel my face breaking into a huge grin.

"Yes, and it sounds perfect," the doctor tells me as I walk closer to Liv and the monitor. She reaches out to clasp my hand and I lace my fingers into hers, sharing the moment.

The doctor continues to press while watching the screen. Following his line of vision, I look over and see the clear outline of a little person. I can see the baby's head, backbone and even the tiny fluttering of what must be a heart beating. I don't even notice I'm crying until the nurse hands me a tissue.

I squeeze Liv's hand before bringing it up to place a kiss on her knuckles. When I look at her beautiful, perfect face, I see she's crying too. We are seeing an image of our child. This is our child, the miracle created by how I feel for this woman.

"She is fucking amazing," I hear Liv whisper and the doctor chuckles.

"Well, actually..." he starts but Liv interrupts quickly.

"She isn't a *she*?" she asks with panic and he laughs again.

"I didn't say that," he reassures. "He *or* she, is being shy." He places a fingertip on the screen and runs it down what I think is a bone in the thigh. "See here? The legs are crossed tight and even when I try to poke and prod to encourage some movement, this little one is determined to keep the secret. I just can't determine the sex. Sorry, Liv."

"Damn! She's already being stubborn," she pouts.

"Then she's just like her Mommy," I point out and laugh when this makes her pout harder.

"But we can still print you out some pictures to show off," the doctor explains, "and the most important thing is the baby looks healthy and right on track."

Maybe I hate him, but I'm too happy to do anything but smile.

Chapter Twenty-Seven: Liv
But Then... They Discover Boys

"We seriously don't know? The doctor has no idea of the sex?" Charli asks again.

"She was being ladylike," I insist. "Maybe she'll end up a good girl, instead of the town slut."

"Well maybe *he* was hiding his junk!" she counters.

"Do you know any man that hides his junk?" I ask and Charli laughs.

"No, I guess you make a good point. They all seem rather proud of it, don't they?"

"And the weird thing is, it's not attractive but they all still seem to think we want to see it. I want a guy that knows how to use it but I'm not going to tell him it's beautiful or build a shrine to it or anything," I tell her as we wipe down the bar and get ready for the evening shift.

"Hand me some more napkins," Charli says. I reach down to

grab the box but groan as I try to stand back up.

"I'm so fat!" I complain.

"You aren't fat!" she insists, "But maybe it's time to stop working so much, Liv. You made good money on that overseas job and I know you haven't spent much of it. Logan and I can cover the rent and even if you just take a few of the photography jobs that don't require you to be on your feet so long, you should be able to manage."

"I'm fine. I like working in the bar. I know I can't for much longer but I'm not ready to give it up yet. I'm slowing down with my photo sessions and mostly taking graphic art jobs that I can do from my laptop at home but the money is good so I can still cover my half of the rent. Don't worry about me okay?"

"It's my job," she insists.

"No, your job is to massage my fat, swollen feet tonight after our shift and buy me some more fucking batteries. Why does pregnancy make you so damn horny? It makes no sense! The desire for sex is supposed to ensure survival of the species, but when you are already in the process of increasing the human population, that desire seems pointless!"

"Complain all you want but when sex becomes a means to an end, it loses some of its appeal. I forget what it's like to spon-taneously jump my husband because he's so hot I can't control myself. My sex life now revolves around ovulation schedules and fertility plans. It's not sexy."

"That sucks, Charli."

"I know. I think we've decided to throw in the towel," she admits.

"What? You're giving up?" I'm so shocked. I know how badly they both still want a baby.

"Yeah. It's making us both crazy. I can't do it anymore. I want a normal life again, that includes a normal sex life. It's obvious this isn't going to happen in the conventional way, so we're going to give ourselves a break and then next year we will talk to the doctors about in vitro. It's expensive and not a guarantee but it still offers me the chance of carrying my own baby."

"That sounds like a great idea. I'll break out my noise canceling headphones and you two can go at it all the time and to hell with what that ovulation chart says!" I know she's disappointed, but I'm so proud of how well she is dealing with it and her plan to move forward. I've noticed the strain between her and Logan lately.

"Oh, I meant to ask earlier but shouldn't we start planning your baby shower? Kelly is insisting she doesn't want one since she still has so much from the twins but this is your first and you need everything."

"A party and everyone has to buy me stuff? Yeah, I'm good with that," I tell her and she laughs as she slaps at me with her bar towel.

"The gifts would be for the baby, not you, smartass!"

We both take a break from our duties and go sit down at the nearest table. We still have an hour before opening, and most things are ready so we can afford a few minutes off our feet.

"Should we ask Ronan to use the bar?" I wonder.

"The bar? Isn't that kind of weird for a baby shower?" She's looking at me like I've grown another head.

"How the hell should I know? I've never even been to a baby shower!" My circle of friends doesn't include any moms except for Kelly and she'd had her twins before I met her.

"What about Verde'? Could we ask Zac?" she suggests.

"Oh, I guess so. Is that weird for me to ask him to use his restaurant?" *I don't want him to feel like he has to do it, but damn,*

I am growing his baby for him!

"Didn't you say his mom, Ginger, wanted to help me with the shower? Let her ask Zac if you don't want to."

"No, that's even weirder. I'll ask him when I go by his place tonight," I tell her.

She cocks her eyebrow at me and starts to smile. "You're going to his place tonight? Hmmmm..."

"Ugh, stop it, Charli. It's not like that. I promised him that I'd come over so we could discuss the birth plan and baby names. I'm trying to involve him in everything but I swear if he argues with me over naming her Scarlett things may get ugly."

"Okay," she laughs, "but what if it's a boy?"

"She's a girl. Trust me!"

"God help you if it is a girl!" Charli and I both turn as Ronan enters the bar, shaking his head in disgust.

"What's wrong with girls? You have a daughter!" I remind him.

"Exactly! So I know what I'm talking about. Oh, it starts out perfect," he says as he comes to join us at the table. He spins a chair around backward, straddles it, and leans forward to share his wisdom.

"They are cute and all smiles and manage to wrap you around their little finger. But then...they discover boys." He shudders while we laugh.

"It isn't funny!" he barks. "They start hanging these posters on their walls with all these punk ass looking teen boys in weird clothes and girlie haircuts. They listen to bands with music that makes you want to shove an ice pick in your ear to end the torture. They want to spend every waking minute on their cell phones and squeal about which boy asked them to the dance. And when the little shit comes to pick up your daughter for a date, you start trying to figure out places you can dump his body if he hurts your baby girl. And after all this, you have to let her go off to college and live on a campus full of guys trying to get in her pants."

I think this is the longest speech Ronan has ever given. I want to laugh but damn he's actually made me feel sorry him. His daughter Kinleigh just finished her second year of college and it's obvious he's struggling with the realization she's now an adult.

"Oh, Ronan..." Charli pats his shoulder consolingly but he's done with the sympathy and jumps up from the chair.

"Anyway," he says, "I've been meaning to tell you girls, Kinleigh is going to come stay with me for a week this summer and help me out with the bar. She's been working on that business degree and it will be good for her to get some hands-on experience."

"Great!" Charli enthuses. "We can't wait to meet her."

"Definitely," I add.

We watch him head back to his office and don't speak until the door closes behind him.

"Poor guy," Charli says and I agree. "I really am excited to meet his daughter, though. He talks about her but I've only ever seen that one picture he has on his desk and she's probably five years old in it. It's great she's finally coming here to see her dad instead of him always going to her."

"Yeah, I think a lot of that is his ex-wife's doing. There's a story there, I just know it, but he sure as hell isn't going to share it. Maybe this Kinleigh will spill," I say.

"You're a nosy bitch," Charli laughs and I don't disagree.

Chapter Twenty-Eight: Zac
It's Time I Come To My Senses

"Come on in," I tell her, opening the door wide.

"Thanks." Liv smiles, even though she looks a little nervous.

"Can I get you anything?" I ask.

"No, I'm good. But thanks," she answers.

Since when did we become so distantly civil with one another? It's not as though we just met. She's carrying my child, and I'm pretty sure that should make us more comfortable, not less.

She enters my living room, looks around the open space and finally chooses to sit on the overstuffed armchair near the window. It's a good choice. It's my favorite place in the room. Joining her, sitting down on the couch across from her, I wait for her to begin.

"Ummm...So, I was wondering if I could ask a favor?" she says while playing with the hammered nails that trim the armrest of the chair.

"Of course. Anything," I assure her.

"Well... Charli and your mom want to have this shower thing. Apparently it's a normal ritual when you decide to reproduce. People will come and eat food and give you lots of shitty advice but they also hand over baby gifts, so that's a win."

"Liv," I laugh, "I know what a baby shower is."

"Right. Of course. Anyway...Charli says we shouldn't have it at the bar. She seems to think it would be an inappropriate location, so she wanted me to ask..." She still can't look me in the eye. I'm not used to Liv being shy about anything.

"You should use the restaurant," I tell her. "You know you are welcome to anything I have. I can have my staff prepare the food. Just have Charli give me the date and time."

"Oh, okay. Thanks. That would be great." She finally looks up and smiles. I smile back. *I don't think I could ever deny her anything.*

"It was pretty damn amazing seeing the ultrasound. My mom started crying when I texted a picture. She's so excited," I tell her.

"I know. Your family has been so awesome about this mess," she says and I tense at her words.

"This baby isn't a *mess*, Liv."

"Sorry! You know what I meant! I'm sure they didn't expect their first grandchild to be illegitimate, Zac."

"Probably not but it doesn't matter to them, or to me, and you know it."

"Yeah, I guess I do."

I'm ready to change the subject. This is touchy ground with us. "So do you have some names picked out?" I ask her, and that makes her give me the smile I love. It's that sexy, mischievous little smile that makes me forget all about our disagreements and tension. Instead, I want to just pick her up and take her to my

189

bed. Our earlier preliminaries on her couch had reminded me how fucking hot we were together and I can't get the feel or taste of her off my mind.

"Well, since you brought it up…" she says huskily as I see her tongue dart out and glide across her full lips and I want to groan in frustration. She knows what she's doing. She's distracting me in hopes of getting her way. *It's working.*

"I want to name her Scarlett," she tells me.

"That's your first choice if it's a girl?" I ask.

"It's my *only* choice. And she is a girl," she insists and I can't help but smile at her conviction.

"Hmmm, okay. Do you have an idea for a middle name?"

"Yes, I want her middle name to be Michaela, for Mikey."

This makes my heart literally slam in my chest with love for this woman. She truly loves my brother like I do. *What will I do if we don't manage to fix what's going on between us?*

"That's perfect, Liv. Thank you."

She smiles, pleased to be getting her way and happy that I like her choices.

"What if we are having a boy?" I ask.

"We aren't," she says.

"But, what if we are?" I ask again and she sighs in frustration.

"I don't know! I guess we can pick something in case but it won't be necessary."

Again, I just want to laugh at her confidence. We spend the next hour coming up with a short list of five names we both like and decide we still have plenty of time to narrow it down to our favorite.

"I guess we should discuss her last name too?" she asks and I tense.

Is there even a question about my child's last name? "Liv, I just assumed the baby would have my last name. That's the way it's done."

"We could always hyphenate. I don't like the idea of my child and I not sharing the same last name."

"You want our poor kid to have to learn to spell two last names and have to write all that shit every time they fill out any paperwork for the rest of their life?"

"Ugh! I don't know! This sucks..." She lies back in the chair and closes her eyes.

"You know, if you would just give us a chance, maybe we could all share the same last name," I remind her.

"Don't start with me, Zac!"

"You are the most stubborn woman I've ever met. Are you aware of that?"

I move closer and sit down on the ottoman near her feet. She props her feet onto my lap and wiggles them in invitation. I notice she's kicked her shoes off. She sighs with pleasure when I gently massage them and giggles when I run my finger softly under her toes.

"Stop it," she complains with a smile, "I'm ticklish."

I move my hands up to her ankles, still slim even though she keeps insisting otherwise. Again, she sighs and I venture even higher. Her mouth opens slightly when my hands have reached her knees and I gently pry them apart.

When they venture even farther north, she actually moans and I'm finding it hard to go slowly. I'm so ready for this incredibly sexy woman moving underneath my hands that I could take her now and be done in mere seconds.

"Mmmmm," she says and I smile.

Next, I place a small soft kiss on the inside of her knee. "This okay?" I ask.

"Fuck yeah, it's more than okay."

God, I love this woman. She knows exactly what she wants and is never afraid to say it. I run my tongue along the inside of her thigh and she squirms and starts to breathe erratically.

"Zac..."

"Yes, Liv...tell me what you want," I encourage.

"I want sex. I'm so tired of wanting sex all the time and not getting it!"

"I'm happy to oblige," I tell her teasingly.

"Thank God! It's been torture," she assures me. "Can we do this regularly from now on? Like, really often? I'm hoping after I give birth I'm not so needy all the damn time but it's partly your fault I'm in this predicament. I think it's only fair you be the one to scratch this particular itch."

She's smiling at me like she thinks her little speech is cute. *It's not.* It pisses me off. I sit back on the ottoman and take my hands off her. She isn't happy about it. *Tough shit.*

"So," I begin, "Let me get this straight. You don't want to try to have a relationship with me? You just want me to be some sort of friend with benefits because you're fucking horny all the time and too pregnant to go out and find some other guy to hook up with?"

"Damn it, Zac! I didn't mean it like that!"

"Well then, please explain what the fuck you did mean, Liv!"

I get up from the ottoman and start pacing the room. I've tried so hard to be patient with her. I've tried to be there for her, made excuses for her, and I really thought she'd come to her senses. *I guess it's time I come to my senses.*

"Look, it's just hard, okay? I'm not ready for us to be a couple but I don't want to go out and hook up with anyone else, okay?" she says.

"Am I supposed to be glad about that? Should I be thankful you don't want to let other men fuck you while you're carrying my child?" I'm yelling at her now and I hate that but I can't help it. This is more than I can take.

"Fuck you, Zac! I've always been honest with you. I'm sorry I can't be what you want right now. Maybe in time..."

"No, Liv, you're right," I say softly. I'm done yelling. "You've always been honest and I should have been paying attention. I can't sit around waiting to see if at some point you want to give me a real chance. I'll be there for my child and provide anything you need while you care for my child but that's it. I won't be at your beck and call because you want sex. I'm not going to come running anytime you want a friend or comfort or reassurances and I'm not going to throw away my chance at finding someone to share my life with. If after all this time, you still don't know if you want me, then I don't want you."

"Fine." She pinches her lips in fury, slips her shoes back on and heads for the door.

"I'll get with Charli about the shower date. Please let me know about any doctor's appointments and if you need help with anything," I say with my back to her.

She doesn't say another word and the only sound is my front door closing firmly behind her.

Chapter Twenty-Nine: Liv
Pink and Candy-Coated

"It's been forever and he still doesn't want to talk to me, unless it's about the baby! I know I pissed him off but it's time he got over it," I complain.

"I don't blame him. That was a bitch move, Liv," Kyle responds.

"Thanks a lot! Whose side are you on?" It pisses me off to know he's right. I can't blame Zac. This is my fault.

"Look, you know I love you. I always will. If you need me, I'm here but that doesn't mean I'm going to agree with every decision you make. You've been stringing that poor bastard along for months. Did you really expect him to wait patiently while you decide if he's worth your time?"

"It's not like that!"

Kyle comes around from behind the bar and puts his arm around my shoulders to give me a quick squeeze. "I get that you didn't mean for it to be like that. I honestly think you're in love with the guy and too stubborn to admit it. But, think about it from his perspective. You jump him the minute he's single, spend a month of phone calls convincing him you're totally hot for him, and then when he wants to make a commitment, you tell him you need space. That's what we refer to as a tease."

"Ugh!" I pull away from him and go sit next to Charli at one of the nearby tables where she's sitting and cutting limes. "I'm not a tease! I got knocked up, in case you didn't notice. A tease doesn't put out. I'm now the size of a planet and I have to think of what's best for this baby! I can't rush into things!"

"Rush?" he laughs sarcastically. "You've been incubating for almost eight months and you're still unable to give him even the hope that you will try and make things work between you. No one would call that rushing into things."

"Do you hear this shit?" I ask Charli but she just continues to concentrate on her lime cutting skills and smiles. "So you agree with him?"

"Liv..." she starts but then flounders like she can't decide what's best to say in the situation I've forced on her.

"Oh my God. You do. You think I'm a tease!" I jump up and start pacing while rubbing the small of my back. I'd thought carrying around big tits was hard but it has nothing on carrying around another human inside you all day.

"No, I don't think you are a tease," she tells me but she's probably just trying to calm me down. "But I know this has been harder on Zac than you realize. He cares for you and you hurt him."

"Shit." I give up. They're right. I was so worried about my own feelings and trying not to get hurt that I'd managed to hurt him. "I'm a terrible person."

"No, you aren't," Kyle insists.

"You just got wrapped up in everything and didn't think things through," Charli adds.

Charli has finished with the limes and walks to the prep sink to wash off the knife and cutting board. Kyle is checking the liquor inventory on the shelves and all the beer taps. Determined to pull my own weight, even though I now weigh a freaking ton, I join them to help finish the prep.

"Damn..." Kyle's voice drops deep and causes both Charli and I to look toward the entrance to investigate its cause. He spends so much time listening to our bullshit, we sometimes forget he is a dude and therefore ruled by his dick.

Walking into the bar is the perkiest Barbie doll of a young woman I've ever seen. She has long blonde hair, big blue eyes, and a mile of deeply tanned legs showcased by a pair of tiny white shorts and platform sandals. She's also wearing pink lip gloss, carrying a ridiculously small pink purse, and straining the limits of her tight pink sweater with a pair of giant knockers. Your first impression might be she's a spoiled bombshell from the sunny west coast but her smile is so big and innocent it just doesn't fit. Instead, you want to go protect her and warn her about all the big bad wolves that would like to take a bite out of her. No wonder Kyle's about to drool on himself.

What in the hell is this girl doing here?

"Excuse me," she says and even her voice sounds like it should be pink and candy-coated, "I was wondering if maybe you could help me?"

Kyle comes out from behind the bar. He is heading her way, wearing his signature panty-dropping smirk, before Charli or I can even react.

"I can help you with anything you need," he tells her and I roll my eyes. I know he's sinfully gorgeous but surely this girl recognizes his game?

"Daddy!" she suddenly shrieks and Kyle freezes.

What the hell?

Ronan has come out of his office and the young beauty in pink has run and jumped into his arms. "Come here, baby girl," he says warmly.

Holy shit. This must be Kinleigh.

Kyle, finally able to move again, turns to face the glare Ronan is shooting him over Kinleigh's shoulder. I should feel sorry for him when I notice Kyle has gone pale and has to wipe beads of sweat off his forehead but I'm a bitch sometimes and I just want to laugh. Letting the boss know you were trying to get into his daughter's pants isn't a good way to go.

"When did you get in, honey? I thought you were going to be here tomorrow?" Ronan asks as he guides her over to one of the small tables.

"I finished up my last exam yesterday so I decided to drive up a day early. I hope that's okay?" She's looking intently at his face and seems a little nervous.

He makes everyone nervous but shouldn't his own daughter be used to his gruff manner?

"Sure, I just wish you told me. I might have been able to give my employees..." again he stares over at Kyle, "a little head's up so they knew to expect you."

"Oh, I'm so sorry. I should have called..." her voice trails off as she looks over her shoulder at our three gawking faces.

"No, it's fine. Really," he assures her.

"Can I meet them?" Her question indicates she wants a round of introductions but she can't take her eyes off of Kyle. Ronan is ready to blow a fuse when he notices and he isn't answering her, so we take the initiative and walk over.

"Hi, I'm Charli. It's so great to meet you," my best friend enthuses as she sticks out her hand in Kinleigh's direction.

"I'm Liv," I say. "Maybe your dad has mentioned me? Obviously, I'm the one that's knocked up. Nice to meet you." Her eyes dart down to my waistline or as I like to refer to it, the equator, and she grins.

"I've heard all about both of you and it's so great to finally meet."

She's so sweet I'm worried I might get a cavity. *How had this little princess come from our rough and gruff Ronan?* Now I'm dying to get a good look at the ex-wife. We'd always assumed his daughter would be a tomboy and tough as nails.

We all watch quietly and expectantly when she turns to Kyle. He won't even make eye contact. *God, I can't wait to give him a hundred kinds of hell about this!*

"Hi," she says timidly, stepping closer to him, but he takes a step back and she flushes.

"Hey," he finally manages, out of necessity. "I'm Kyle... and I have a lot to do." With that, he turns and leaves for the back storage room. We all stand around like idiots trying to figure out what in the hell just happened.

"So..." Charli says to fill the awkward silence. "How long is your visit, Kinleigh?"

She reluctantly takes her eyes away from Kyle's departing backside. *You can't really blame her. Kyle's ass is hot.*

"Oh, I'm just here for the week. I'm doing a summer program, interning at an office back home, and it starts a week from tomorrow so I can't stay any longer." Her answer is coherent but she's obviously still flustered.

"Oh, then you'll be here for Liv's shower this weekend!"

Charli tells her. "You are welcome to come if you want. Of course, you don't have to but..."

"I'd love to! Thanks!" Kinleigh is beaming and she looks so damn cute.

Charli has always been casually cool with her Chucks and torn jeans. I've always been considered the girlie one because of my love of dresses and heels but I still rock an edge too. Next to this girl, I almost feel like a dude.

How can anyone wear so much pink and not look ridiculous?

"All right," Ronan cuts in, "let's go get you settled. You can follow me over to my place and we can hang out there this evening and catch up. Kyle and the girls can handle the bar."

Kinleigh looks at the doorway Kyle had just disappeared through. "I don't mind staying here at the bar with you, Daddy. I'd love to help out."

I know exactly why she wants to stay. I also know exactly how Ronan will respond.

"No. Let's go home. There's plenty of time to deal with..." he pauses and looks in the same direction she is, "the bar later."

Chapter Thirty: Liv
What Have I Done?

"Oh my God! Guess what?"

Charli comes running out of the kitchen and toward me at breakneck speed. She's barely able to stop herself before crashing into the chair I'm currently occupying like a giant slug. I feel as big as a house, my ankles are classified as "cankles" and I'm so tired my eyelids feel like they have lead weights attached to them. My belly is currently having a spaz attack as little Scarlett does her daily workout. When I went to the bathroom five minutes ago, my face looked so shiny I had to dive into my purse for emergency powder.

They promised glowing. Where in the fuck is my glowing?

At this point, nothing is going to excite me. "What, Charli?" I ask as I stifle a yawn.

"So, Logan just called to let us know that Kelly can't come to the shower today!" she says while wearing a grin that is so big I swear I can see her back teeth.

Why exactly is she excited that Kelly can't be here? I thought she liked her. "So, that's good news?" I ask.

"No, but the reason she can't come is good news! She's at the hospital having the baby!"

Okay, that is good news but unless I'm the one about to give birth, I don't have the energy to muster up much enthusiasm. "Great. That's great. Good for her. I'm starving. When do we get to eat?" I ask. A girl has to have priorities. I am eating for two, as they say.

"Ugh," she complains, "You are impossible. The guests should start arriving soon but I'll go grab you a snack if you really can't wait. Zac made enough food for us to feed the whole block but I have no idea what most of it is. I'll bet you'll love it."

I wince when she says his name. I'm sure she noticed, but to spare me any embarrassment, she ignores my reaction and tells me she'll be right back before disappearing to get the snack.

Zac, as promised, has allowed us to use his restaurant for the shower today and Charli and Ginger have gone all out. Every table is draped in an ivory cloth with centerpieces of blue and pink hydrangeas. There are clear glass plates and napkins of pale green. The backs of all the chairs have been tied with oversized chiffon bows that alternate between pink and blue. The whole dining room is pastel overload.

"Wow, I love it!" I hear as I turn toward the entrance to see which guest has arrived early.

Ronan's daughter is spinning in circles to take in the room. Her buttercup yellow dress has a full skirt and it dances along with her movements. Of course, this girl loves the décor.

"Thanks," I say with a smile. She looks like she should be a decoration. "I can't take any credit for it but I'll accept your praise on behalf of my best friend and the baby's grandmother. I'm glad you could join us," I tell her.

"Oh, I'm so happy to have been included. You just met me and you're so sweet to let me come."

Wow. She thinks I'm sweet. I know this impression won't last but I'll enjoy it for now.

"I hope you don't think I'm being too pushy," she says, "but I made something for the shower. I'm not trying to step on any toes and I know the baby's father provided the food, so you don't have to use these but..." She looks down shyly and I notice she's carrying a large shopping bag.

"What do you have?" I'm genuinely puzzled. What could this girl have brought that would cause her cheeks to turn pink?

"I really, really like to bake. I'm not a professional or any-thing, but I wanted to..." Again, she looks down toward the bag in her hands.

"Kinleigh, just tell me what you have," I'm trying to stay po-lite but I'm getting tired of her stalling.

Setting the bag down, she pulls out a large pink box and opens the lid. She tilts it in my direction and I see the box has cardboard dividers to protect the contents from sliding around. It's a good thing too because the cupcakes crowded in there are little masterpieces.

"You made those?" I say a little too loudly. I guess it's rude that I sound shocked but damn, they look better than the ones on that Cupcake Wars show I watch.

"Yes. It's my hobby," she admits. "I'm always baking cakes and pies and cookies... but cupcakes are my favorite."

"If they taste even half as good as they look you're amazing."

"Oh, you are so sweet to say that!"

So far, so good. She still thinks I'm sweet!

"You can just take them home with you if you want. You don't have to put them out," she says shyly.

"I want them right in the middle of the dessert table," I assure her. "But first, I need a sample. Bring me one over!"

"Okay," she smiles and I swear she's so beautiful it's enough to make me question my sexuality for a minute. "I have lemon chiffon with raspberry buttercream, pecan praline or peanut butter truffle."

"Why are you getting a business degree?" I ask. "You should have gone to pastry school. They sound heavenly. I'll take one of everything."

She looks so pleased when I cram a cupcake into my mouth, barely chewing, in order to stuff more down my throat. The girl has some mad skills with a cupcake. Charli was impressed too when she joined us and immediately added them to the dessert table.

It isn't long before the guests start arriving, so I slip my shoes back on to my poor feet and make the rounds. Tired or not, I'm not going to let anyone think I don't appreciate them coming. It's obvious my little Scarlett will be well loved.

"I think it was a great idea to ask everyone to give the baby a book instead of wasting money on cards," Ginger tells me as she sits down in the chair next to mine.

It's almost time to start opening gifts and she's offered to keep a list so I can make sure everyone gets a thank you card. My moms are sticklers about writing thank you cards and I know better than try to make excuses. Unless the zombie apocalypse strikes tomorrow, those cards will be in the mail on Monday.

"It was actually Charli's idea. You know how much she loves to read and she'll make sure this baby has a fully stocked library before her first birthday."

"I'm so glad you have each other. It's such a special friend-ship." What she's saying is true, and I agree completely, but her face has a tension that doesn't go with her words.

"What's wrong, Ginger?" I ask.

"I was just thinking of Zac."

Shit. I should have known. Why did I ask? Her son is this baby's father and we are barely speaking right now. "I'm sorry," I whisper as I fiddle with my hair and look around the crowded room. I know it's my fault we aren't together. I kept asking for more time and he was right to give up on me.

I feel her hand rest lightly on my shoulder and when I get up the courage to look at her face, she is smiling. It's a little sad but there's no anger.

"Honey, you don't have to apologize. He's my son and I love him. I just want him to be happy and I thought that you..." she pauses and considers how to continue. "Well, I just thought that you two could have been happy together but I guess it's not meant to be. It's no one's fault. We can't help who we love."

"Umm..." What do I say to that?

I do love Zac. It's always been Zac, from the very first moment I saw him. How do I explain that I'm scared he doesn't feel the same? How can I tell his mother that with Zac I'd had the hottest sex of my life, that I feel better anytime he's near, that I love his pas-sion for life, and I die a little each day we are apart?

She'd probably gross out over the sex thing and then tell me to beg him to try again. But how can I be sure he wants me in the same way and isn't just with me for the baby's sake?

"Gift time!" Charli's voice gives me the reprieve I need and I gladly take the first wrapped box she hands me.

"Hell, yeah!" I yell as I pull out a pair of tiny leopard print shoes with black marabou trim and a rhinestone on the ankle strap. I plan to train my daughter from birth to appreciate the beauty of shoes, especially heels. How early can their ankles handle a nice little wedge sandal, I wonder.

"The receipt is taped to the bottom of the box," Madison, the waitress Ronan hired while I'd been away, tells me. "You know... just in case, she's actually not a she?"

Everyone giggles at my frown. I'd made my stance on this issue perfectly clear.

I open bags and boxes until it all becomes a blur. A few people had taken my intuition to heart and purchased lacy things, bows, and pink dresses but for the most part, I receive gender neutral sleepers, toys, bath items, and diapers. Charli and Logan purchased the crib and Zac's parents gave me a stroller and car seat combo so I'm feeling pretty set for this whole baby thing.

"Only two more gifts," Ginger tells me as she places a small blue gift bag in my lap with a wink. "This is from Mikey."

After pulling out all the red tissue paper, I find a little blue onesie with an attached red cape and the Superman logo on its front. I can't help but smile. That kid loves his superheroes.

"You know he is as stubbornly sure this baby is a boy as you are that it's a girl."

"Even after you explained her middle name will come from his name?" I ask. I'd been sure that would win him over to my side.

"He just smiles and says the baby is a boy and will be his nephew and friend, no matter what we say," she tells me.

"Well, I love the gift anyway. I can always add some rhinestones and glitter when she gets here."

"We'll see..." Ginger says with a smile.

She nods her head at Charli and they announce to all the guests that they are welcome to enjoy the desserts and punch now. Ginger is about to walk away when I grab her sleeve to stop her.

"I thought you said there was one more gift? I don't want to hurt anyone's feelings. What did I miss?"

"I just thought..." She compresses her lips and then nods to herself as if making up her mind about something. "Here. This is from Zac. I just think you might want to open it while alone."

Handing me a small square package, wrapped in pale green paper with cream polka dots and a large bow, she takes a deep breath, turns away from me and walks toward the kitchen to escape. Nervously I fidget with the taped edges, unsure of what to do.

Deciding to take Ginger's advice, I head for the restaurant's vestibule area since everyone else is near the dessert table raving about Kinleigh's cupcakes.

I sit down on the teak bench in the secluded space. Sliding my nail under the tape, I pull back the paper and see the small book nestled inside. Reading the title, I begin to cry.

This is my fault.

I've made a huge mistake and not only have I ruined my chance for happiness but I've just taken away the chance for my precious baby to be raised in a single home with two loving parents.

"Liv?"

Charli joins me cautiously, waiting to see if I want to be alone. I don't. I want my best friend. Even more, I want the man I've fallen in love with. I want the man that no longer wants me.

"Oh, Charli...what have I done?"

She immediately sits down beside me and pulls me into her arms. I hand her the little book and wait for her to read its title.

"Oh, Liv...I'm so sorry."

We sit together silently as my tears fall in steady streams for several minutes. When I'm finally able to pull myself together enough to go back to the dining room, I stow the book away in my purse. Before it drops down into the depths of my giant bag, I run my finger over the words one last time and whisper the title to myself.

"**Mommy and Daddy Always Love You!** *How to explain to your child that you can love them without being in love with each other."*

Chapter Thirty-One: Zac
Too Old For These Games

"I feel a little sorry for the poor bastard!" Logan says, shaking his head in sympathy.

"Yeah, he's seriously outnumbered," I agree.

"I mean, I'd love a daughter of course!" Logan asserts, "I'd love to have any baby at all..."

I slap him on the back and hand him another beer. "You will," I tell him with complete conviction.

"But...all girls? Scott has three daughters now, plus Kelly. He will be living in a house with four females. Poor bastard," he says again.

"And what about once they start dating?" I add and we both shudder.

"Liv is convinced our baby is a girl and I'd be lying if I said the thought of a little red-haired beauty that looks like her mother doesn't do funny things to my heart. But when I start thinking about boys looking at my daughter, or wanting to take my daughter out...I want to buy a gun."

"Have you seen Liv with a gun? She never misses. She'll scare the hell out of anyone trying to mess with your kid."

I smile, knowing what he says is true. Liv and I aren't together but I know how remarkable she is.

"I'm not trying to get all personal and shit...but, are you okay? Charli said you and Liv are..." Logan runs his hand through his hair in frustration. "Fuck! I don't know what to say. I'm just sorry, okay?"

"Thanks," I tell him but I don't want to talk about it so I'm glad he drops it.

"I better get back to the apartment now," Logan says as he stands and reaches for his coat he threw over the back of the chair. "The shower should be over and I need to put that crib together. You should see the instructions! It's like a damn novel. I'm sure I can figure it out easier without them."

"Good luck," I tell him.

"You don't think I can do it?" he asks with a laugh.

"I bought the same crib to have here at my place and it took me three days to figure it out."

He groans. "Shit."

"Yeah, and no offense but you aren't exactly the handiest of people," I remind him.

"Maybe you could come over and help me out?" he asks hopefully.

"I would but... I don't think Liv wants me there."

"I think she does. She's just too damn stubborn to admit it."

"Well, I'm sorry. I'm done chasing after her and waiting patiently for her to figure out what she wants. If she wants me, it's up to her to let me know and even then I'm not sure I trust her enough to try anymore. I'm too old for these games, Logan."

"I know. I get it."

I lean against the wall that connects my living room to the entryway. "I don't mean for you to be caught in the middle of our shit."

"It sucks but there's nothing to be done about it. It will work out," he assures me.

"I hope so," I say but I have my doubts.

"Okay, well I really do need to go," Logan says as he turns away and heads for the door.

"Sure. Tell Charli hello for me."

"Will do. Bye." He throws a quick wave over his shoulder before leaving.

"Bye."

Once Logan has closed the door behind him, I walk down my long hallway to the small room adjacent to mine. I open the door, as I do several times a day, and smile.

I've painted the walls a soft gray and put the white crib on the long wall across from the door. There is a matching chest of drawers and a long dresser with a changing pad on top. I've also added a bookcase and a glider in the corner. Next to the crib is a large shopping bag with two sets of bedding. One is pink and white, and the other is navy blue and gray.

In just a few more weeks, this will be my baby's room.

I'd asked Logan to come over today to hang out and share a couple of beers but I'd need his professional services too.

"I don't practice family law!" he had reminded me with a deep frown.

"I know but this should be fairly simple."

"Let me recommend someone better suited to handle this," he tried again.

"Please. I don't want to go to a stranger and explain my situation. You know it would turn into something a lot bigger than it needs to be. Just draw up the papers for me, Logan." He didn't look happy about my request.

"What is Liv going to think?"

"I'm sure she will see how important this is and understand I'm doing it for her."

At that point, Logan had laughed. I understood perfectly. Liv probably won't see this as the generous offer I mean for it to be.

"Okay, I'll do it," Logan finally relented. "It's your head that will roll if she doesn't agree."

I hope Liv understands why I need to do this. I'm not trying to hurt her or cause any problems. I really hope we can stay friends at least and work together to create stability. This will protect us both.

Chapter Thirty-Two: Liv
It's Almost Time

"Hell, no!" I screech as I throw the packet of papers back at Logan.

"Liv, if you'll just listen to me..." he tries.

"I'm not divorcing him, we aren't even married, so why in the fuck do we need a custody agreement?" My voice has gone up at least an octave. As I pace up and down the length of the bar, I realize this is the fastest my giant body has moved in months.

"It's a good idea for both of you, Liv."

"No, it's not! This is MY baby! She will live with me! He can see her anytime he wants and I guess I'm okay with her staying overnight once in a while...eventually...but we aren't dividing her time into percentages and making this a business contract!"

"He just wants the standard visitation schedule. It will make it easier for both of you to plan your lives. You'll both know in advance when you have the baby and be able to make plans for vacations or special events. You will need a holiday schedule too. And what about child support?" Logan reasons.

"I don't want his damn money!" I'm starting to hyperventilate and my back is hurting like a bitch.

"It's not for you, Liv. It's for the baby. He wants to make sure she has everything she needs." Logan is doing his best to sound reasonable. I know I'm frustrating him but I don't care.

"I can and will provide everything my child needs," I say with indignation.

"Charli," Logan turns to his wife in desperation, "will you please talk to her?"

"Liv, maybe you should just..." Charli starts.

"No!" I scream at her, and then I have to sit down. I feel kind of lightheaded and Scarlett is kicking like a Radio City Rockette. I don't think she likes me being pissed off.

"What in the hell is going on in here?" Ronan yells as he enters the bar from the back entrance. He looks as pissed as I feel. "I can hear you shrieking from out in the parking lot!"

Kyle also joins us, from Ronan's office. Kyle has been suspiciously absent lately. He's usually in the middle of everything that goes on in the bar but for the last week, all he's wanted to do is hang out in the office, handling the business end of things.

"Zac wants to take my baby! How do you think I should react, Ronan?" I yell up at the mountain of a man I call my boss and consider my friend.

With that, his face softens and he comes to sit near me. "What are you talking about? Zac is a good guy, Liv. I don't see him trying to take this baby away from you."

"Well, he is... sort of," I say but my anger is losing steam. I'm mostly scared now.

"You guys leave us alone for a few minutes," Ronan commands and I watch my friends scatter. "Now, you calmly tell me what's going on, Liv. And don't you forget that I said *calmly*."

"Okay," I snuffle, suddenly overcome with emotion. *Damn these pregnancy hormones!*

"Zac asked Logan to draw up legal papers that make sure he will get his share of time with the baby. Doesn't he trust me? Doesn't he know that I want him to be a part of her life?"

"Look, I'm sure he does know that. We all do. But when kids are involved things get very emotional, as you've shown today. Sometimes in anger or fear we make bad decisions. If Zac were the one immediately getting custody of this baby and he was just telling you that he promised to share it with you, would you be okay with that? What happens when he gets married and there is a stepmom in the picture? Life changes and circumstances change and this type of document just makes sure no one can let those changes rob them of what they deserve."

Oh my God.

When Ronan mentions Zac one day getting married, I almost double over in pain. My gargantuan stomach won't let me double over of course but my head had fallen forward and my heart had seized in my chest. *Zac can't marry someone else!*

"Um...Ronan?" I say softly.

"I know, Liv. It's hard to think about. I just watched Kinleigh drive away and head home. Even now, with her all grown up, I think back to how it was when she was little. When her mom, Amber and I were going through the divorce, it was hard trying to figure it all out. And then when she..." Ronan is looking off, lost in his memories, but I need his attention now!

"Ronan!" I practically shout, right next to his ear.

"What?" he yells back. "Liv, you need to..."

"Ronan, shut the fuck up!" He's used to my potty mouth but

he doesn't like it.

He scowls at me. "What the hell is your deal? I'm trying to help you!"

"I do need your help. My water just broke," I say calmly since he is now listening to me.

"What did you say?" His voice drops so low I can barely hear his question and his face is deathly pale.

"Ronan, can you drive me to the hospital now?"

"Charli! Logan! Kyle! Get your asses down here now!" He shouts loud enough to wake the dead.

"Damn, Liv! Did you piss on the floor?" Kyle asks from the doorway. "I'm not cleaning that up. It was bad enough I had to take care of the puke the night of the bachelorette party but I'm not..."

"What puke?" Ronan roars.

"Oh, shit," Kyle says.

"Guys! Focus!" I demand as Charli and Logan join us.

"Kyle, quit acting like a little bitch. Clean up my mess and then meet us at the hospital. Logan, go grab your truck. Charli grab my suitcase. Ronan, hold my hand. It's almost time to meet Scarlett."

Chapter Thirty-Three: Liv
I've Changed My Mind

"Oh my God! He's your doctor?"

"Charli, can you put your tongue back in your mouth before your husband gets jealous?" I ask sweetly as she laughs and Logan scowls.

"But he's just so... Maybe I need to switch to his office? Does he handle infertility?" I know she's trying to distract me and is getting the bonus of agitating her husband.

"Okay, Liv," Dr. Will says when he enters the room again, carrying my chart. "Everything looks good. I know your due date is still a couple of weeks away but the ultrasound and tests show the baby is fine and fully developed so we will let the labor proceed. How are you feeling?"

He's smiling at me and is extremely gorgeous, but right now all I want is drugs. *I need drugs. This shit hurts.*

"How am I feeling?" I ask sarcastically. "I'm feeling like a ten-pound demon from hell is trying to crawl out of my vagina. How are you today, Doc?"

He laughs, which makes me want to kill him, and then makes a note in my chart.

"I'll order something to help take the edge off. First pregnancies usually take a while but I'll check in regularly."

And with that, Dr. Will leaves me with my useless friends that are not authorized to provide me with the hardcore shit I want. I keep hearing how childbirth is such a beautiful and natural process. I will politely disagree with that sentiment.

Since arriving at the hospital, I've been made to wear a paper gown with no panties. I've had no less than ten medical professionals take an up close look at my hoo-hah and even go so far as to insert cold, gloved fingers to check my dilation. I've been stuck with IV needles, told I can't have anything to eat even though I'm starving, had a catheter inserted, and even asked if I felt like I needed an enema.

No thanks.

"Liv, honey, we're here!" My door swings open and I thank God my gown is down and the covers are up. My moms come barging in as Logan and Charli step out.

"Really?" I reply and for once, my mom lets my sarcasm go by without comment.

"You know, it seems like yesterday we were here to have you," Mom tells me, fighting back sniffles.

"Yeah, when you popped out, it looked like Carol's vagina was inside out but you were the prettiest thing I've ever seen," Momma D adds. Of course, Mom hits her shoulder and tells her to shut up.

I just laugh. It's a gross visual, she is my mother after all, but it's still funny. Then I realize my body is about to do that very same thing.

Holy shit. Is my vagina going to be inside out? Will it ever be normal looking again? Damn it, am I going to have to have sex in the dark from now on because my vagina looks like some kind of alien creature? Maybe I need to ask for a C-section? Maybe a bikini area scar is better than a fucked up vagina!

"Liv? Can I talk to you?" Charli asks as she peeks her head back into the room.

"I'm not going anywhere," I quip but she doesn't even smile.

"We're going to grab some coffee," Momma D says, "Want some ice chips?"

"I want a Dr. Pepper and a Snickers bar, please," I tell them.

"Not happening, sweetheart. Sorry. Just ice chips," Momma D responds.

"No, thanks," I pout.

"Okay," Mom adds. "We love you, baby."

"I love you too," I say as they close the door behind them.

"What's up?" I ask Charli once we are alone.

"We can't get hold of Zac," she tells me.

"What?" I'm trying to stay calm but panic is a real threat. Another contraction hits hard and Charli has to wait for it to pass before she can continue.

"We've been calling and texting but he isn't answering."

"Did you try his parents?" I ask. *Surely, this is an obvious suggestion?*

"Yes. We got hold of Ginger and she is heading up here now. She is sending James and Mikey to Zac's house to find him. Maybe he's just napping or something and didn't hear his phone."

I can tell she is grasping for excuses. He always has his phone. He's told us all a million times how he sleeps with it right next to the bed and checks it constantly to make sure he knows as soon I go into labor.

Well…I'm in labor. Where in the hell is he?

"We'll find him, Liv. He'll be here," she tries to reassure me.

"Whatever. I don't even care," I say petulantly but we both know it's a lie. Maybe the biggest lie I've ever told. *I do care. I need him with me.*

"I'll just go and…"

"Ow!" I grab Charli's hand and squeeze as another contraction hits.

"Liv? Another one? You just had a contraction. Don't they seem a little too close together?"

I lie back and pant a little. "I don't know. It just seems like it's never going to end."

She tries to get her hand back. "Let me get the doctor…"

"No! Don't go! Don't leave me!" I beg. This really sucks. It's like the worst menstrual cramp of my life multiplied a hundred times.

She pushes my damp hair away from my forehead. "Okay. I won't leave. I'll text Logan to come here."

Continuing to hold my hand, she uses the free one to message him. Within seconds, he's joined us.

"Any luck?" she asks him but he just shakes his head and they both look worried.

"Ohhhhh…" My groaning pulls their attention back to me. I'm hurting too badly to even cry out now. I will no longer believe that those women that cuss and scream during labor are in real agony. When the pain gets real, you don't have the energy needed to scream.

I need Zac. Where is he?

"Logan," Charli says softly, "go find the doctor. Now."

Glad to be escaping, he practically bolts out the door.

"Zac," I say hoarsely. "Find him, Charli. Please!"

She presses a cool, damp rag to my face and murmurs comforting things but I can't focus on what she's saying. My consciousness has just expanded to encompass everything and simultaneously shrunk down to this one single-minded need to bring my baby into this world.

"Okay, Liv, it's almost time."

I hear Dr. Will in the room now and there are nurses scurrying busily but I need Zac. I only want Zac.

"Honey, do you want me to roll the big mirror in here so you can watch the birth?" A round-faced, older nurse asks me in a soft, soothing voice.

"Hell, No!" Charli and I both scream in unison.

"Okay, Liv, listen to me," Dr. Will says, "You just jumped from four centimeters to ten centimeters in about twenty minutes. This baby is ready to say hello. When I tell you to push, you push."

"Owwww..." I moan, "You said I could have the epidural! Where's my epidural?"

"It's too late now. But you can do this," he says as if he knows.

He doesn't know shit! I can't do this! I've changed my mind!

"Zac!" I scream when the next contraction hits.

"Almost time...okay, Liv...Push!"

"Umph...Zac!"

I bear down with all I have and choke back a sob. *Where is he? He promised he'd be here. I can't do this without him!*

And then, my heart lifts at the most beautiful thing I've heard in my life.

"I'm here! Liv, I'm here! Baby, I'm here!"

Chapter Thirty-Four: Zac
Perfect

"Baby, I'm here," I promise in a soothing tone as she clings to my hand, hard enough to cut off circulation to my fingers. I use my other hand to push back the damp red strands of hair that are stuck to her forehead as she bears down for another contraction.

"Oh oh oh," she moans softly. "Where in the fuck were you, Zac?" she whispers as the contraction lets up.

"This is it, Liv! Last push," the doctor promises and she closes her eyes to bear down.

"I can't. I just can't," she cries.

"Yes, you can," I tell her. "Liv, you are the strongest, bravest, most stubborn woman I know. You can do anything."

"Zac, I'm so sorry!"

"Shhhh, don't worry about that. Let's just get our baby here."

She just nods and concentrates, too intent on what must be done to make another sound.

"That's it! Congratulations, Mom and Dad!" Doctor Whatever-His-Name-Is says as he cradles a screaming, slimy little bundle of pink with a thick patch of matted, dark hair.

My baby. He's holding my baby.

"Can I hold her?" Liv croaks as I bend down to gently kiss the top of her head. "I want to see her. Is Scarlett okay, Dr. Will?"

"Your baby is perfect, Liv. But..." the doctor begins but I cut him off in panic.

"But, what? What's wrong?" I practically yell.

Dr. Too Good Looking smiles. "There is nothing wrong with your baby. *HE* is perfect. Scarlett is a boy."

I start to laugh. I can't help it. "Let me see my handsome Scarlett, Doc," I tease. "You chose the perfect name for our son, Liv." She scowls, but I can't stop. "He looks just like a Scarlett."

"Oh, shut the fuck up and give me my son," she pouts.

The baby is laid on her chest and his cries stop as he starts rooting around. Liv's face relaxes and she's more beautiful than she's ever been as she tucks her chin down against the top of his head. My throat swells and I feel a sting in the corner of my eyes. I cough self-consciously, trying to keep my composure in front of Dr. Pretty Boy as he turns to address Liv's business end.

What is he doing now? Isn't he done? The baby is here! He's got no more business down there!

"Oh, Zac," Liv whispers, drawing my attention back to her and my precious son. "He is perfect. He is the most perfect thing I've ever seen." She snuggles him in even tighter and carefully inspects each little finger and toe. I see tears running down her cheeks and sliding onto the baby's head. I think my heart is going to burst. I love them both so much.

"You did good, babe," I tell her.

"No, we did good. He looks just like you, Zac."

"He has your eyes," I tell her.

"I'll let you guys have a few minutes," the doctor says as heads for the door. "You did great, Liv. Congratulations to you both."

"Here, let me take him," one of the nurses says as she reaches for the baby.

"No! He's mine!" Liv pulls our son tighter.

"I'm not stealing him, dear," she assures her calmly. "We just need to check him out and clean him up. I'll bring him back as soon as I can."

"Oh...okay." Liv reluctantly hands him over. I give my son a kiss on the top of his sweet head and we all laugh when he cries out. Liv and I watch together as he's placed in the clear-sided bassinet and wheeled out.

"I love him so much, Zac."

"I know. I do too."

"And..." she looks away and I see her swallow deeply. "I am so sorry I've been such a bitch. I was scared."

"I know. It doesn't matter."

"It does! It does matter!" She looks back to me and her eyes are glittering with tears. "I pushed you away. I didn't think you loved me. I was so sure you wanted a baby so badly that you would pretend you loved me for the baby's sake. I just couldn't believe you actually loved me as much as I love you!"

"You love me?" I whisper in disbelief.

"Yes. I love you so much I can't imagine my life without you. I love you so much that when you find someone else, someone that loves you in the way you deserve, I might die from it. I love you so..."

"Shut the fuck up, Liv," I tell her with a huge smile before bending down to kiss her with all the love and passion I've had to hold back for the past eight months.

"Congrat... Oh!"

I break the kiss and we both turn to the doorway. Standing there, with identical smiles of shock and joy, are all of our family and friends.

"I told you my Liv's baby was a boy!" Mikey calls out from the center of the crowd.

Chapter Thirty-Five: Liv
Who Knew?

"So, where were you?" I ask. The arrival of our son had prevented his explanation earlier but I'm determined to get some answers now.

"Huh?" Zac yawns and stretches from where he's uncomfortably folded in the small reclining chair next to my bed.

"Where were you when I was brought to the hospital? You promised to have your cell with you at all times and no one could find you," I complain. Even though he'd made it in time, barely, it had been too close.

"Oh! Well, we were a little short staffed in the kitchen, so I was helping them out. I'm running around everywhere trying to make sure everything is perfect."

"Of course," I smile, acknowledging how particular he is about his restaurant.

"So, I'm draining a large pot of fusilli and…"

"A large pot of what?" I ask in confusion.

"Fusilli...it's pasta."

"Oh, please continue."

"Okay, so I'm lifting up this giant pot and my hands are pretty high up and my phone slips out of my apron pocket and into the colander with all the hot, wet pasta. I freak out when I realize the phone is dead, so I leave almost immediately to run to the mall to that cellular kiosk to get it replaced."

"You are kidding," I say in true astonishment.

"Liv, I haven't let that phone out of my sight since finding out you were pregnant. I leave it on the bathroom counter when I shower. The one time, in eight months, that it isn't working is when our son decides it's time to arrive."

"Damn, he's already a little mischief maker, isn't he!"

"What did you expect?" he asks. "Have you seen his mother?"

"Well," I drawl, batting my eyes and reaching out for his hand, "I've seen his father and I'm completely mad for him."

Our fingers intertwine and he leaves the chair to come and sit on the side of my bed. We both look over at the tiny sleeping baby in the bassinet near us. My heart swells and I feel complete.

Who knew my little parasite would make me feel like this?

"What are we going to call him?" Zac whispers before gently positioning himself next to me in the bed and sliding his arm under my head. He then kisses my temple and I sigh in perfect contentment.

"Winchester?" I ask, hopefully. It's a gun and the family name of some really hot brothers on my favorite TV show. *What could be better?*

"No," he chuckles.

"Remington? Maybe, Remy for short?"

"Does he have to be named after a firearm manufacturer,

Liv?"

"Glock?"

"NO!"

"Okay, okay! Damn, I just want him to have a badass name. It will increase his chances of survival when the zombies attack." *This is totally legit reasoning, in my opinion!*

"If you have your way, he will be an expert marksman before kindergarten anyway. I don't think we have to worry about his survival skills."

"True," I concede.

"How do you feel about Benjamin? It was my grandfather's name."

"Benjamin? Ben? Hmmm..." I think it over and look at his earnest and expectant face. *I love this man. I love our son. I'm happier than I thought possible.*

"Well?" he asks.

"I like it. Benjamin Michael Reynolds. It's perfect."

The smile he rewards me with is instant and amazing. It's also hot. My baby's daddy is very, very hot.

"Reynolds? Really?" he asks hesitantly and I feel guilty for ever denying him this.

"Yes. Definitely."

He rolls to his side and pulls me against him, careful of my still tender body but close enough for him to give me a kiss that makes me think waiting the six-week recovery period is going to be a bitch.

"Damn! This is the kind of shit that landed you two here in the first place!"

We separate and look toward the new voice in the doorway. Logan is laughing and Charli is positively beaming.

"I'd tell you to get a room but I guess you have one already,"

Logan adds, obviously thinking he is funny. "It's more expensive than any hotel I know of though and the food sucks."

"Oh, shut up, Logan!" Charli laughs as she punches him lightly and comes to stand near the bassinet. "Congratulations. He is so beautiful."

She lightly strokes the top of Ben's head and we all laugh when his mouth purses and he starts making little sucking motions. He's already discovered he a big fan of eating.

"I won't argue with you," I tell her, "and little Ben can't wait to be spoiled by his Aunt Charli and Uncle Logan."

"Ben?" she asks with a big smile. "I love it! And I will love spoiling him."

"He will be great practice too," Logan says with a wink at Charli and she blushes.

Wait...what? "What are you talking about, Logan?" I'm trying not to get too excited in case I misunderstood.

"We're pregnant, Liv," Charli tells me, with tears now falling freely down her face as she continues to pat Ben's back. "We are going to have a baby!"

"Oh my God! Are you kidding?" I squeal as I try to jump up from the bed and belatedly realize that is a terrible idea. "Owwwww!"

"Liv! Are you okay?" Charli rushes to my side, practically forcing Zac off my bed.

"I'm good. Episiotomies suck. Stitches on your hoo-hah are a nightmare!" I lie back against my pillow and take deep breaths.

"You have stitches *where*?" Zac asks quietly and I notice both he and Logan are looking a little pale.

"Oh, for fuck's sake, Zac! It's not going to look like Dr. Frankenstein got hold of it. Dr. Will is a perfectionist. If you're lucky, maybe he added a stitch or two for you," I wink but he doesn't seem to find the humor in it.

Men. They are such pussies.

"The parents are all dying for their turn to see the baby again. We'll leave and send a couple more in," Charli offers.

"Okay, thanks," I tell her. "You're the best hooker I know."

"I love you too, whore."

Epilogue: Kyle
No Problem At All

What the hell happened to all my friends? They used to be cool!

"Kyle? I'm so glad you made it!" Charli pulls me into one of her tight hugs but I can't get very close considering she looks like she swallowed a bowling ball.

"Sure. I wouldn't miss your housewarming party, babe," I tell her and I'm rewarded with that smile I've always loved.

"It means so much to Logan and me." She pulls me into a large open foyer and starts yelling to everyone that I've arrived.

Within seconds, Logan is slapping me on the back and I hear a commotion coming from the direction of the living room.

"No, Ben!" Liv yells, scooping up the crawling rugrat off the floor and handing him over to Zac. "Your son eats all day long and still feels the need to put everything he can get his grubby little hands on into his mouth!" she complains but she's laughing and planting kisses all over the baby's chubby cheeks.

"Welcome to pure chaos," Ronan murmurs as he passes behind me. "I need a beer."

"I'm with you," I agree, following his lead.

Once we have successfully escaped into the kitchen and pulled cold bottles of beer from Charli's refrigerator, we lean on the counter in shared misery.

"How long have you been here, man?" I ask.

"Too long. I got the full tour of Charli and Logan's new house, along with a full explanation of all her decorating choices in the nursery. I had to hold little Ben and listen to all the details of Liv and Zac's upcoming wedding. I also had to pull those twins of Scott and Kelly's out of the damn tree in the backyard after they got stuck. Kelly couldn't reach and Scott was off changing their new kid's diaper."

"Shit."

"You have no idea," he says with a shudder before taking another long pull from the almost empty beer.

"How long do we have to stay at this thing?"

"I'd have bailed already, except I'm waiting for Kinleigh to arrive."

"What? Kinleigh is coming?" I try to sound natural but the break in my voice doesn't go unnoticed and Ronan narrows his eyes.

"Yes. My daughter should be here soon, with cupcakes apparently."

"Oh," I say and clear my throat. *Is it getting hot in here?*

"She's decided to move down here and help me at the bar. Is that a problem, Kyle?" he asks with a raised eyebrow.

Shit.

"No," I tell him. "No problem at all."

Coming Next

Kyle's Story: "Wreck"

.

I am fucking ridiculous. I need to grow a pair and quit hiding in the damn pantry!

Just as I've finally convinced myself it's time to man up and rejoin the party, the door to the large, walk-in pantry opens and the light from the kitchen shows me a silhouette I instantly recognize.

"What are you doing in here?" she asks softly.

"Uh...I was looking for the extra paper towels. Charli said Ben spilled his drink and I... Ummm...I just..." We both know it's a lie.

"You were looking for paper towels in the dark?" she asks and I hear her doubtful amusement.

Shit. Can't she just let me off the hook and leave?

"What are you doing here?" I ask her.

"Wondering why you snuck off."

Shit.

"I didn't sneak off," I insist feebly.

"Uh huh," she giggles and I feel that familiar tightening. She does this to me. I know I need to stay away from her but it's so damn hard.

"What do you want, Kinleigh?" I groan.

"You, Kyle. I want you."

Acknowledgements

From Stacey:

Calvin... thank you for sharing the crazy chaos we call our life. I love you more. Without our son Justin, his wife-Krysten, and their sons Carson and Easton... our daughter Kayla, her husband-Ronnie, and our "soon to be arriving" grandson, Brixton... our son Steven and finally our daughter, Hannah... we would have more time, more money, and far less fulfilling lives.

From Karen:

Donnie... I love you. Always have and always will. We may not be perfect at everything but when I look at the men our sons, Shawn and Tyler, have become... I know we've done something very, very right.

From Stacey & Karen:

Once again, we want to thank our awesome "book girls". Amber Byford, DeAnna Ben, and Carol West... you've truly helped us to make our dream a reality.

To Laura Hampton, we thank for your fast and accurate editing and your belief in our stories.

To our Beta Readers (Kathy Price, our "Book Girls," Donnie, and

Kayla) - Thanks for the feedback and help in making this story everything we wanted it to be.

Special thanks and big sloppy kisses to our Donward... once again your edits saved the day.

HUGE, grateful thanks to the best (if somewhat unwilling) for-matter. Tyler Bell you are priceless.

About The Authors

Once upon a time, these two hookers became best friends...

Stacey Brandon and Karen Bell both live in the same small Texas town on the Gulf Coast, are happily married and the proud Moms of awesome kids. Stacey owns and runs a photography studio and Karen designs and sews her own children's clothing line. They met over fifteen years ago when they decided to turn one large professional space into a single home for both businesses.

Well, that's all the boring facts expected to be included in an "about the author" page, right? The reality is so much more fun. Stacey and Karen and their families spend holidays together, travel together... and generally turn every situation into something crazy and chaotic. They are both fluent in English, Sarcasm and Profanity and have decided the irrefutable proof of their best friend status is how often people assume they are "together" when in public. The poor husbands are good sports about it... and might even encourage this misconception at times for sheer entertainment value.

When Karen battled cancer... and kicked its ass... in 2014, they learned to value every day and quit worrying about what others think. Do what you love! Karen is happy to take advantage of the situation though. She loves to remind everyone she "had the CANCER, dammit!" and now she can always and forever claim the last brownie ;)

www.ingramcontent.com/pod-product-compliance
Lightning Source LLC
Chambersburg PA
CBHW020603180626
46810CB00007B/2629